# HIGH COUNTRY AMBUSH

# AN AMERICAN ADVENTURE SERIES

# HIGH COUNTRY AMBUSH

## LEE RODDY

Published in association with the literary
agency of Alive Communications, P.O. Box
49068, Colorado Springs, Colorado 80949

Published by Bethany House Publishers
A Ministry of Bethany Fellowship, Inc.
6820 Auto Club Road, Minneapolis, Minnesota 55438

Printed in the United States of America

**Library of Congress Cataloging-in-Publication Data**

Roddy, Lee, 1921–
    High country ambush / Lee Roddy.
       p.  cm. — (An American adventure ; bk. 9)
    Summary: When Hildy Corrigan's unemployed father announces the
family is moving away from their friends just before Christmas, 1934, Hildy
feels anger and pain; but adventure beckons when she and friends track a
stolen horse in the Sierra Nevada Mountains, where a dangerous convict
and a snowstorm threaten their lives.

    [1. Adventure and adventurers—Fiction. 2. Sierra Nevada (Calif. and
Nev.)—Fiction. 3. Depressions—1934—Fiction.
4. Moving, Household—Fiction. 5. Christian life—Fiction.] I. Title.
II. Series: Roddy, Lee, 1921–
American adventure ; bk. 9.
PZ7.R6Hi    1992
[Fic]—dc20                          92-24497
ISBN 1–55661–287–7              CIP
                                   AC

To

Elmer Winger

for his friendship and

the very special contribution

he has made to our lives

# CONTENTS

# Chapter One

## Terrible News

Hildy Corrigan suddenly tensed, then quietly reined in her horse. The unexpected sound of bawling cattle and men's subdued voices warned her that something strange was going on in the dense fog.

"Whoa, Buster," she commanded softly. She tipped her maroon flat-crowned hat back over her waist-length brunette braids and cocked her head to listen. Her blue eyes probed vainly through the wet, dismal fog. It clung stubbornly to the gently rolling hills and sagged heavily into the gullies.

Dismounting quietly, Hildy dropped the reins, knowing the old buckskin gelding would stay ground-hitched. Walking on tiptoes through the winter-brown grass, she moved warily toward the sounds.

When she made out the forms of two men on horseback, the twelve-year-old girl froze. The riders were herding half a dozen whiteface steers into a stake-sided truck. The men wore heavy jackets against the December cold. A third man on foot, similarly dressed, ran through the barbed-wire fence, which had been cut and pulled aside. He hazed the last animal into the truck and raised the ramp so it became a gate.

He turned to the horsemen. "Let's get out of here before this fog lifts."

The taller rider chuckled. "Ain't much likelihood of that happening before noon, Zane."

"Don't argue!" Zane snapped, starting around the left side of the truck. "Get those horses in the trailer. Split up like we planned and meet me later."

The shorter man eased his sorrel mare from the field onto the dirt road beside the trailer, which was partly hidden behind the truck. "You better get a good price this time, Zane, or . . ."

"Or what, Smokey?" Zane challenged, whirling to glare at the rider.

Smokey hesitated, then lowered his eyes. "Nothin'."

Zane glanced up at the tall rider. "What about you, Al? You got anything to say about how I handle this?"

Al shrugged, drawing his unshaven chin down into the warmth of his ancient Mackinaw. "All I want is my share."

"You'll get it," Zane assured him, turning and disappearing around the far side of the truck.

Hildy's heart leaped. *They're stealing Brother Ben's stock!* She turned toward her mount just as he neighed to the other horses. Hildy's heart leaped into a full gallop.

She glanced back just as the shorter cattle rustler shouted. "Hey! Somebody's watching us!" He kicked his mare into a gallop toward Hildy.

She turned and dashed back to Buster. Grabbing the reins, she leaped into the saddle with an easy motion. She pulled the buckskin's head around hard, gave him a free rein, and drummed her heels into his flanks. In spite of his twenty-three years, Buster broke into a gallop. His coarse mane stung Hildy's face as she leaned low across the horse's neck. "Faster, Buster! Faster!"

Keeping the reins loose, she raised her right arm and peered back under it. The fog had erased any sign of her passing, but a darker, moving shadow farther back warned Hildy that her pursuer was closing fast. Far behind, she could hear Zane's angry shouts.

As Buster topped a hill and started down the other side, he suddenly broke stride. Instantly, Hildy realized what her desperate ride was costing the old gelding. "Easy, boy!" she said quietly, reining in. "I forgot."

She loosened her feet in the stirrups and swung off quickly as the horse stopped, breathing hard from the short run. She glanced around in the fog for a possible hiding place. The open, rolling hills offered nothing, but she spied a small gully to her left.

She darted to it and paused at the brink, anxiously looking for a way down to the rocky bottom twenty feet below. She held her breath to listen, but there was no drumming of pursuing hoofbeats behind her.

*He's turned back!* Hildy thought with a sigh of relief. She retraced her steps to the buckskin. "I'm sorry about running you so hard, Buster," she whispered, patting his neck. "I got so scared I forgot you're no colt." She took the reins and stepped ahead of the horse. "We've got to get to Brother Ben's and tell him what's happened. But we'll both walk so you can rest."

The horse seemed no worse for his short, wild run when Hildy led him down the long, eucalyptus-lined gravel driveway to Ben Strong's low, Spanish-style ranch house with the cook shack, bunkhouse, and barn beyond. The 85-year-old former U.S. Marshal and Texas Ranger stepped out of the screened-in back porch in the main house.

"You're back early," he said in his easy drawl.

"Some horsemen stole your whitefaces!" Hildy blurted out. "One chased me, but Buster and I got away."

The old ranger's piercing blue eyes widened in surprise and an angry scowl wrinkled his brow. "When? Where?" he asked crisply, giving his drooping white walrus moustache a flip with the back of his right forefinger. He was six feet four inches tall, wore a white cowboy hat, sheepskin coat, blue jeans, and tan cowboy boots.

Hildy hurriedly explained what had happened. She finished by adding, "I forgot how old Buster was and ran him too hard. When I realized that, I stopped. He seems all right."

"That's fine. Did you get a good look at those men?" he asked with obvious concern.

"Sort of." Hildy briefly described the three rustlers as best she could, adding, "Oh, I also heard their names: Al, Smokey, and Zane."

"Zane?" The old ranger repeated sharply, then shook his head. "No, couldn't be." He excused himself to phone the sheriff.

*What couldn't be?* Hildy asked herself as she hurried outside. She led Buster to the barn, unsaddled him, and turned him into the corral. She rushed back to the house to ask what the old ranger had meant.

Because Ben had been a widower for many years, he had picked Hildy up at her home that morning to dust and clean for him. She did that periodically. Sometimes she and her cousin, Ruby Konning, also cleaned house for Matthew Farnham, Lone River's only banker, whose wife had been crippled by polio. The Farnhams didn't need the girls' services today, so Hildy planned to visit with Ruby after finishing at the old ranger's home.

Hildy was saving to buy gifts for Christmas, which was little more than two weeks away. So far, she had saved a whole dollar, a lot for the Depression year of 1934. As usual, after finishing her chores, Hildy had saddled Buster for an enjoyable ride across the ranch, only to run into the rustlers.

Hildy entered the living room and sat in one of two rawhide-bottom chairs. They had red and white cowhides for backs. A large black Bible and stacks of Western magazines rested on the coffee table made of a spring wagon seat. The walls were lined with artists' sketches of cowboy life, rusted spurs, branding irons, and other mementos of a long, outdoor life.

Still wearing his coat and carrying his hat, Ben joined Hildy. He sat down rather stiffly on an old-fashioned sofa. A blanket with bright red and black Indian design was draped over the sofa's high back.

Hildy asked, "What did you mean a few minutes ago when you said, 'No, it couldn't be?' "

Ben frowned and ran an age-spotted hand along a full head of pure white hair. "I was reminded of a man I arrested about twenty years ago named Zane Vernon."

"You think he's the same man I saw?"

"Not likely. The Zane I arrested fled to Texas, where he's still serving a life sentence for a double murder he committed there." The old ranger paused, a shadow of pain flickering across his face.

"What's the matter?" Hildy asked anxiously.

"Zane Vernon was the only prisoner who ever escaped from me. That was the worst blemish on my long career as a lawman. But what still hurts—besides the fact I never caught him again after he escaped—was that he ambushed me. I'd have died if it hadn't been for Buster."

"Really?"

Ben's eyes clouded. "That's why I've kept Buster all these years."

"What happened?"

Ben sighed softly. "Even though it was such a long time ago, it still hurts to talk about it." The old man stood suddenly. "Maybe someday I'll tell you, but right now I want you to show me where you saw those men. I'll fix the fence, then drive you to Ruby's."

When the fence was repaired, Ben held the passenger-side door open for Hildy to slide into the leather seat of the 1929 Packard Victoria. It was a big yellow car, with black fenders, a brown canvas top, and whitewall balloon tires mounted on bright red spokes. The matching spare tire in a brown covering rested in the well at the base of the right front wheel. The elegant car reflected Ben's success despite hard times.

"Too bad a man can't track trucks and trailers," he commented. "But all I can do now is ask questions of the butchers in Lone River, in case those three rustlers try to sell the meat to them. Well, your cousin's expecting you, so let's go."

The fog had lifted, but the sky was still totally obscured when the old man and the girl arrived at the bunkhouse where Ruby Konning and her father lived. It stood outside the small rural community of Lone River, nestled on the most easterly part of California's great San Joaquin Valley where the foothills of the majestic Sierra Nevada Mountains begin.

At Hildy's knock Ruby opened the bunkhouse door. She was a year older and an inch taller than Hildy. As usual, Ruby wore her favorite tomboy clothing—boy's overalls and a faded blue workshirt. She turned her hazel eyes on her visitors.

"Howdy, y'all," Ruby greeted them in her Ozark Mountain accent. "Daddy'll be back directly. He's up at the ranch house, a-talkin' to the owner. Come on an' make yorese'fs to home."

"Much obliged," the old ranger replied, "but some cattle rustlers hit my place this morning, so I've—"

"Cattle rustlers?" Ruby interrupted. "I ain't never heerd o' sucha thing 'ceptin' in Ol' West hist'ry."

"This Depression has brought them back with some modern tricks, like trucks. Anyway, Hildy can tell you all about that. I've got to run. *Adios*, ladies."

The cousins waved to Ben. Then Hildy, bursting with excitement, blurted out the morning's experience. She ended by telling what Ben had said about being ambushed and how Buster had saved his life.

The girls discussed the episode until they'd exhausted the subject. Then Hildy produced a Bull Durham sack she'd found. She opened the drawstring and shook out a silver dollar. A few grains of tobacco fell out with the money in her palm.

"I already got a gift for everybody except Molly. What do you think I should get her?" Hildy asked, extending the coin for her cousin's inspection.

"Yer gonna spend ever' bit on her, or waste part of it on Spud?"

Hildy rankled at the implied dislike for her friend. "Please try to get along with him."

"Why should I? He makes me mighty tahred with his two-dollar words!"

Hildy started to defend the boy, then sighed, knowing it was useless. She explained, "He's like Brother Ben, Mr. Farnham, and all my friends at school and church. They're sort of like my extended family."

"Thar ye go, usin' a two-dollar word—*extended*. I reckon ye l'arned that from ol' Spud."

Hildy bit her tongue. She and Ruby were more than cousins; they had been best friends all their lives. They'd sometimes had minor disagreements, but since they'd met Spud last June, there had been periodic tension between the girls.

"Let's not quarrel," Hildy said evenly. "Okay?"

Ruby nodded, but added, "Ye kin fool yorese'f if'n ye want, but ye cain't fool me! That ol' boy means a lot to ye!"

"So do you, and Brother Ben, and Mr. Farnham," Hildy replied. "You're all special. So's Lone River." She loved the small, rural, San Joaquin Valley agricultural community. She added, "This is the only place in my life where I've felt like I belonged. I think this is where I'll find the 'forever' home I've always wanted. Now, let's change the subject."

They did, but there was still a slight strained feeling between them when Ruby's father, Hildy's Uncle Nate, dropped her off late that afternoon at the tarpaper shack where Hildy lived with her family.

"Hi, Molly," Hildy called. "I'm home." She walked through the living and dining rooms to the lean-to kitchen. "Where are the kids?"

Hildy's stepmother closed the oven door on the wood-burning stove and wiped flour-covered hands on her apron. She was a nice-looking woman with brown eyes and light brown hair, showing a few streaks of gray.

"They're playing in the barn. Your father wants to see you right away. He's at the woodpile."

There was something about Molly's somber tone that disturbed Hildy. She hurried outside toward the California hip-style barn. She could hear her four younger sisters laughing inside the haymow. Hildy followed the ring of her father's ax to

the north side of the barn where he was splitting almond firewood for the family's kitchen stove.

Hildy stopped well back from the ax and pulled her winter
coat tightly about her against the chill. "Daddy, you wanted to
see me?"

He glanced at his oldest daughter, nodded, then drove the
single-bitted ax into an old tree stump he used as a chopping
block. His eyes, blue as her own, startled Hildy because they
were bloodshot. She had never seen her father cry, but there
was a sad, discouraged look on his face that concerned her.

He stood by the dark, rough-barked almond wood he'd been
splitting. He was bareheaded, the white of his forehead showing
where his hat usually rested below his dark hair. Beads of perspiration glistened there in spite of the crisp weather.

He removed his gray cowboy hat from a nail sticking out of
the barn wall. "We're moving," he announced bluntly.

Hildy had heard those dreaded words countless times, but
she'd never gotten used to them. "Oh, Daddy!" she groaned.
"Not again!"

Hildy had been born in a sharecropper's cabin, then been
moved from state to state. Since last summer, she had lived in
a split-log house in the Ozark Mountains, a California tourist
cabin, a tent, a barn, and now a tarpaper shack.

"I've got no choice," he said, picking up his frayed coat from
a pile of wood.

"I hope it's to a real house this time."

"Yes, it's a house, but . . ."

When he hesitated, Hildy looked up in sudden alarm at the
grim line of his mouth. "But what?" she prompted.

"We're moving away from Lone River."

Hildy jerked backward as though she'd been slapped.
"Where?" There was anguish mixed with surprise in her voice.

"To Flatsville."

"No!" Hildy was so shocked the word exploded from her
lips. It was bad enough to leave her best friend and all the Lone
River people she'd come to love, but to move a hundred miles

away to the place disparagingly called "Okie Town" was un-thinkable.

"We've got no choice," her father repeated, his voice hard-ening. "I've lost my riding job here, and I've not been able to get another one. But I heard about a job driving a tractor in Flatsville, so I went over and was hired. I start in two weeks."

"Two weeks?" Hildy's voice slid up in anguished pain. "That's just before Christmas!"

"I know."

"Daddy, you can't mean it!"

His jaw muscles twitched and his voice became stern. "If there was any way in the world we could stay here, we would. I'm doing what I must. Now, I wanted to tell you first so you could prepare your little sisters—Where you going?"

Hildy didn't answer. She turned and rushed blindly out of the barn into the fog, her eyes burning with sudden, bitter tears.

# CHAPTER
## TWO

---

# UNEXPECTED TROUBLE

Hildy rushed past her startled stepmother and into the small, unheated bedroom she shared with her eleven-year-old sister, Elizabeth. Still in her coat, Hildy sprawled face down on the army cot, her emotions a storm of cruel shock, deep pain, and bitter disappointment.

Hildy's thoughts whirled into memories of the people who had made her the happiest she'd ever been. *I can't leave Ruby! We've been best friends all our lives. Or Spud. He's the most special boy I've ever known! And what about Brother Ben, Mr. Farnham, and all the others?*

There had been very little happiness in anyone's life in the fifth straight year of the Great Depression. It was a worldwide problem, but a very personal one to Hildy and her family. Now the hard economic times had delivered another harsh blow.

It was bad enough to move away from Lone River and all the good things it represented. But to move to a community known for its high crime rate and extreme poverty was even worse.

Hildy moaned silently within her tortured self. She raised

her head from the blue-and-white striped pillow ticking. There were no sheets or pillowcases.

Hildy sat on the edge of the cot and closed her eyes. *Lord, I can't stand the idea of moving away from everyone, especially to Flatsville. What will I do?*

For several seconds, Hildy sat in expectant silence. Then she made a decision. She hurriedly reentered the lean-to kitchen. "Molly," Hildy announced, "I've got to talk to Ruby."

Her stepmother again closed the oven door on the wood-burning stove. "But you just saw her."

"I need to see her again."

"You can do that tomorrow at Sunday school."

"It can't wait! Besides, now that her father has his own church, she goes there, not where I go."

Ruby had never cared for *religion*, as she called it, so she rarely attended church with Hildy, but now that Ruby's father was preaching in his own church, she reluctantly went there out of loyalty to him.

Molly wiped her hands on an apron and walked over to face her stepdaughter. "Hildy, I know that moving away is hard on you, especially just before Christmas. But it has to be done, so you may as well face it and go tell your sisters. They'll take it better coming from you than from me or your father."

Resignedly, Hildy nodded and headed for the barn.

Elizabeth was the first of the towheaded sisters to react. She sat down on a bale of hay and shrugged. "If it's got to be, it's got to be."

Hildy was disappointed at such placid acceptance, but she wasn't surprised. Elizabeth was always practical.

Martha's face puckered as though she were about to cry. Hildy knelt and put her arms around the eight-year-old. "Maybe we can get Daddy to change his mind," Hildy said hopefully.

Sarah, nearly six, shook the bangs out of her eyes and almost screamed. "You promised! You promised!"

Hildy frowned, not understanding. She sat down on the bale of hay beside Elizabeth and lifted her youngest sister, three-year-old Iola, into her lap. Iola was too young to grasp what was being said, but Sarah's wailing had upset her.

Elizabeth spoke up, "Hildy, remember right after Mama died and we were living in the Ozarks? You were trying to be the mommy for us all because Daddy was off somewhere looking for work, and all of us were crying."

Hildy's face clouded with the sad memory. She nodded, her brown braids brushing against her shoulders. She remembered her words as though she'd said them yesterday: *Our daddy'll come back and take us off someplace where we'll never have to move again. No more sharecroppers' cabins. No more tumbledown shacks in the Ozarks. Most likely, we'll move to California. We'll get us a nice house—a big one. And there we'll be together always. It'll be our "forever" home.*

"You promised!" Sarah screeched, banging her tiny fists against Hildy's legs. "You promised . . ." she ended in tears.

Hildy's own tears formed a quick, hot film across her eyes. She reached out and encircled the sisters, holding them close. Controlling her voice with difficulty, she said huskily, "I know I promised us a 'forever' home. And someday we'll have it. But right now—well, maybe I can help Daddy find a job in Lone River; then he won't move away."

"Of course!" Elizabeth exclaimed brightly, drawing back from Hildy's arms. "You know lots of people, Hildy. They can help find a job for Daddy. Then we won't have to move!" She jumped up and climbed the wooden ladder into the haymow.

"Where you going?" Hildy asked.

"I've got some hard candy hidden up here," Elizabeth explained. "It'll make everybody feel better."

Hildy almost laughed in spite of herself. Elizabeth, who had known hunger with the rest of them, had long ago started saving some of her precious food or other goodies. She hid them in case there was nothing to eat in the house.

Maybe the celebration was premature, but now there was hope. Hildy said with forced cheerfulness, "First, I'll talk with

Brother Ben at church. He hires cowboys. Then I'll talk to Ruby and Uncle Nate."

"Talk to Mr. Farnham, too," Elizabeth suggested, climbing down the ladder with one hand. The other held striped red-and-white hard candy. "He not only owns the bank, but he has ranches too. Daddy said so. Maybe Uncle Nate'll give you a ride out to the Farnhams' place."

Elizabeth handed a piece of candy to each of her sisters while giving Hildy a shy look. "You'll get to see Spud too," Elizabeth said softly.

Hildy felt a sudden warm surge inside. Spud's father was a drunk who beat the boy, so Spud had run away and become a young hobo. He and Hildy had met and become friends. Recently the banker and his wife had temporarily become Spud's legal guardians.

Hildy turned abruptly away from her sisters so they couldn't see that her face was slightly red. "Eat your candy," she said.

The next morning Hildy, Elizabeth, and Martha rode to Sunday school with a neighbor. The girls' father never attended church. Molly stayed home with the two youngest sisters and their baby brother, Joey.

At the white-frame church with its steep front steps, Elizabeth and Martha dashed off to talk with friends in their Sunday school class. Hildy waited under the leafless sycamore trees by the curb until Ben Strong arrived in his Packard.

"Brother Ben," she said, approaching him as he got out of the car, "any news on the cattle rustlers?"

The old ranger stepped from the running board to the street and retrieved his white hat from the front leather seat. "I called the sheriff's office again this morning. Another ranch lost some stock north of town, but nobody saw anything. The rancher found his fence cut and several head of steer missing. Apparently those rustlers are just getting started in this area."

Hildy wanted to know more, but she had other matters on her mind. She fell into step with Ben as he started climbing the church steps. "Daddy says we're moving to Flatsville in a couple of weeks."

The old ranger looked down from his great height, his brow puckered in a frown. "I thought your family liked it here in Lone River."

"We do, but Daddy hasn't been able to get work since he was laid off from his riding job. He found work driving a tractor at Flatsville, but I don't want to move."

Ben Strong stopped halfway up the stairs, breathing hard and wheezing slightly.

It surprised Hildy. She had never seen him do that before. "You all right?" she asked with concern.

"Just winded, I guess," he said, puffing slightly. He added, "You know that your father has to go where he can get work."

"I know, but I hope somebody will give him a job, maybe as a cowboy, so we can stay in Lone River."

"I see." The old ranger was still puffing and wheezing a little.

Hildy waited, hoping Ben would volunteer to hire her father to ride at one of the ranches she knew he owned.

"Hildy," he said at last, looking directly at her with piercing blue eyes, "I'd like to help, but . . ."

"But what?" she prompted as he hesitated. Her heart had already started to plunge into despair.

"Well, I wasn't going to say anything just yet," Ben replied slowly, "but I'm thinking of selling out and moving into town."

Hildy jumped as though she'd been stuck with a pin. "Why? Is something the matter?"

"The doctor says I should slow down a little."

Hildy wondered when he had been to see the town's only physician. She frowned. "Any special reason?"

"Like Buster, I'm not a colt anymore."

Hildy sensed he wasn't telling her everything, but that thought passed as he continued.

"Sorry I can't help. Maybe Matt Farnham can."

"I'll try him later," Hildy said, keenly disappointed. She added, "Please take care of yourself."

*I've got to talk to Ruby and Uncle Nate!* Hildy told herself as she headed downstairs to her Sunday school class. *And Mr. Farnham and Spud. If they don't know of a job for Daddy, I don't know what I'll do!*

Hildy was so deep in her own thoughts that she didn't really listen to the lesson. She didn't feel like talking to anyone in her class, so she escaped upstairs after the closing prayer.

She deliberately sought the last row away from her friends so she could be alone in the church service. She noticed Brother Ben taking his usual seat on the left front side near the altar rail. He stared straight ahead when the small choir sang.

*That's not like him,* Hildy told herself with a frown. *I hope there's nothing seriously wrong.*

Hildy's thoughts drifted back to her own problem, so she didn't really hear Pastor Hyde talking about preparing Christmas baskets to be distributed to the needy. She only half heard the announcement about Christmas caroling the next week.

*Why do I care?* Hildy wondered. *I won't be here unless my daddy can find a job real fast.*

Hildy tuned out the preacher's sermon, but she noticed when he turned away that the shiny back of his blue serge suit was wearing thin. His pant cuffs were frayed, and the heels on his black shoes were run-down.

*Preaching doesn't pay much,* Hildy decided, *but at least Brother Hyde's got a job.*

She thought briefly about trying to talk to him after church, but decided that wouldn't be practical. Everyone would want to shake his hand and talk, and he or his wife had probably invited someone to lunch in the adjacent parsonage.

*What am I going to do?* Hildy moaned inwardly. *I can't move away, especially at Christmas!*

She was so deep in thought that she didn't realize the service was over and people were greeting one another on their way out. Hildy slipped past an usher and into a small, empty Sunday school room at the back of the sanctuary.

After a while, she peered back inside. Everyone was gone except the old ranger. He started walking toward the back of the church. As Hildy watched, he staggered slightly and reached to grab the back of a pew for a second. Then he walked again up the slanting aisle toward the front door.

Hildy hurried toward him. He looked pale and little beads of perspiration stood on his forehead. "What's the matter?" Hildy asked anxiously.

"I . . . don't know," he said weakly. "Got the sweats, I guess. And I'm having trouble breathing."

"I'll get somebody." Hildy turned back toward the inner doors.

"No, please don't disturb anyone."

Hildy paused, looking uncertainly at him.

He said quietly, "I'll rest a minute, then go home."

"Please let me get someone . . ."

"I'll be all right," he said huskily.

Then suddenly he staggered and fell heavily to the floor.

# CHAPTER THREE

# THE DOCTOR'S DIAGNOSIS

A hastily summoned church usher rushed Hildy and the stricken old ranger to Lone River's only medical facility. Gruff old Dr. Carter, called "Doc," was the community's sole physician. He had met them at the small clinic, which served for emergencies. Townspeople were building a hospital with the financial aid of banker Matthew Farnham, but that wouldn't be ready for months.

More than an hour later Hildy was alone in the waiting room, alternately pacing the hardwood floors, praying silently, and fighting off depressing thoughts. *O Lord, don't let Brother Ben die!*

She shook her head to rid herself of the idea and stared down the silent hallway as she had done countless times before. The sharp, unpleasant medical smells drifted to her nostrils from the examining rooms.

*What's taking so long?* Half an hour ago the waiting room was crowded with church members who'd heard about Brother Ben, and had come to be near him. Hildy asked the usher to have her neighbor take Elizabeth and Martha home and explain to their parents what had happened. Brother Hyde volunteered to take Hildy home later.

That was before Doc came out and asked everyone except Hildy and the pastor to leave. It was too soon to have any real news about Ben, and there was nothing the people could do but pray. The pastor urged them to go elsewhere to do that, then asked an usher to phone Matt Farnham, Ben's good friend, because the old ranger had no nearby relatives.

Moments ago, Doc had motioned for the pastor to come with him. That made Hildy fear the worst, but there was no one to whom she could turn for comfort.

*I wish Ruby were here.* Hildy stopped pacing to stare absently out the clinic's large front window, which faced the community's main east-west street. It also served as a highway connecting the county seat fifteen miles to the west and mountains some sixty miles to the east. The fog had lifted somewhat, but the threat of its return discouraged driving, and traffic was light.

A stake-sided truck passed in front of the clinic, heading east. Hildy barely noticed until she witnessed an old Nash sedan run the stop sign beside the clinic. It was too late for the truck to stop. The two vehicles collided with the sound of broken glass and crunched metal.

Hildy pressed her nose against the cold window glass to get a better look. The truck driver leaped from his cab and rushed toward the car. Its driver had fallen forward, landing on the horn so it sounded continuously. The man's hat had fallen off, revealing a bald head with a ring of gray hair above the ears and around the back.

*He must be unconscious!* Hildy decided, grabbing her coat off the hat tree and dashing outside to help. The cold December air was a sharp contrast to the warm clinic, but Hildy barely noticed. She sprinted down the sidewalk toward the accident.

The driver of the Nash slowly straightened up, relieving Hildy's anxiety. The truck driver in heavy jacket, boots, and a cowboy hat jerked the car door open.

"You dumb old coot!" he roared, grabbing the bald-headed man by the shoulders and yanking him violently from behind the wheel. "I'll teach you how to drive!"

"Stop that!" Hildy cried, recklessly running up and tugging on the younger man's arm. "He's hurt!"

The truck driver whirled and glared angrily at Hildy, his right arm poised to drive a blow into the older man's face. "This is none of your business, girlie!" the beefy man growled. "Now get away!"

Hildy hesitated, suddenly aware that there was something familiar about the man and his voice. She glanced back at the stake-sided truck. *It's the same one!* the thought seared through her mind. *He's the man who stole Brother Ben's stock! Zane—that's his name!*

The cattle rustler's eyes narrowed in sudden suspicion. "Why're you looking at me like that?"

"Uh . . ." Hildy hesitated, glancing at the driver of the Nash. "You need a doctor," she said.

The man gingerly felt his forehead where it had struck the steering wheel. "I'll be okay."

"Are you sure?" she asked.

He nodded as the truck driver looked closely at Hildy. "Do I know you?" he asked warily.

Hildy swallowed hard. "No." She backed out of reach.

Behind her, she heard the clinic's door open and the pastor call, "Hildy, is everyone all right?"

Zane answered, "Everything's fine." He dropped his voice to a whisper. "You two get out of here, fast!"

The driver of the car protested, "We have to call the police and file an accident report—"

"No cops!" Zane interrupted. "Don't either of you file a report or say anything about this. You hear me?"

Without waiting for an answer, he turned and sprinted to the truck. He scrambled into the high cab, pulled around the crumpled Nash in the intersection, and drove off at full speed. Hildy could hear his right front fender scrape against the tire.

She also noticed that the truck was empty.

Brother Hyde hurried to the accident site. "I'll take care of him, Hildy. You go inside. Brother Ben's asking for you."

The examining room door was open, so Hildy called out softly and heard the old ranger invite her in. She entered fearfully. He stood in front of a small mirror, buttoning his shirt.

"Brother Ben!" she exclaimed. "Are you all right?"

He turned and smiled at her. "I'm fine now. Doc's letting me go home."

"What'd he say? What happened to you at church?"

He reached out and lightly placed both hands on her thin shoulders. "There's nothing for you to get upset about. Doc said I can drive home."

"By yourself?" Hildy jerked her head so hard her long brown braids swung out, hitting the examining table. "You can't! Come home with me! You need somebody to look after you in case . . ." She left the sentence unfinished.

A gentle, understanding smile touched the old ranger's lips. "Hildy, thanks for your concern, but I need to get home. I've got to make arrangements for getting Buster up to a friend's ranch in the high country."

Bewilderment spread over Hildy, making her blink. "I don't understand."

Ben retrieved his coat from a hook behind the door. "I was born in 1849, the year gold was discovered in California," he said in his slow, soft drawl. "I'll be 86 years old next month. That's a powerful long time for a pair of lungs to work."

"Lungs?" Hildy's eyes opened wide. "You got TB?" Instinctively, she wanted to step away, because tuberculosis was common and known to be contagious, but she forced herself to stand still.

Ben shook his head. "It's not that. Doc found a lump in the lymph glands under my armpit. He says that probably means I have cancer inside, but he'll have to run some tests to make sure."

"Oh, Brother Ben!"

"Don't look so stricken, Hildy. I've always faced things head on. Even if he's right, he says I'll be around awhile yet—long enough to put some things in order, like providing for Buster. Since you like him so much, I thought you might want to help me move him to where he'll have good pasture and an easy time the rest of his life. Will you help me?"

When Hildy nodded, Ben put his arm around her shoulder and they walked slowly down the hallway. "Good."

Hildy wondered if he knew she was weeping inside.

As they entered the waiting room, Hildy saw the pastor and doctor talking. Through the clinic's front window, Hildy saw that the Nash and its driver were gone.

Hildy started to tell the old ranger about seeing the man called Zane. But just then she saw a familiar Pierce Arrow pull to the curb. Matthew Farnham, the banker, slid out from behind the wheel. As usual, he was nattily dressed in a three-piece dark suit with a large gold watch chain stretched across the vest.

But Hildy's eyes focused on the passenger, and her heart gave a joyful leap. *It's Spud!*

The boy bolted from the car, wearing his usual aviator cap with goggles, in honor of his hero, Charles A. Lindbergh, who had flown the Atlantic alone from New York to Paris seven years before.

The flaps on Spud's cap fluttered about his freckled face as he sprinted across the sidewalk and burst through the clinic door. The banker followed him at a more moderate pace. Spud was strongly built with wide shoulders, a narrow waist, and hands too big for his body. His reddish hair curled out in rebellious tufts from under his cap. But it was the 14-year-old boy's green eyes that always made Hildy feel a little strange. It was a feeling she had never known before meeting Spud.

The boy looked up into the old ranger's face. "You okay?"

"Yes, Spud," Ben replied with a smile. He turned to the banker. "Matt, I'm sorry about the news you must have heard that brought you into town in all this fog. But as long as you're here, let's you and I talk a couple of minutes. Hildy, would you and Spud mind?"

Hildy didn't mind—not at all. She pulled her coat tightly about herself and suggested she and Spud take a walk.

"Uncle Matt and I came as fast as we could after the usher phoned us," Spud explained, opening the door of the waiting room. "What happened to Ben?"

As they walked down the street, Hildy briefly told about Ben collapsing at church and the doctor's diagnosis.

Hildy answered Spud's questions as best she could, including the old ranger's request for her to help move Buster to a friend's ranch. "Oh!" Hildy exclaimed. "That reminds me, I forgot to tell you something else that happened since I last saw you."

She told about the cattle rustlers stealing Ben's livestock, and about seeing the outlaw leader's truck hit by a car in front of the clinic.

When she had finished, Spud asked, "Did you get the license number of the truck?"

Hildy's eyes opened wide. "It never occurred to me! How could I have been so thoughtless?"

"It's quite logical. You had much more important things to occupy your mind, like Ben's health."

Hildy smiled. "Thanks for being so understanding." She turned and looked back. "I didn't know we'd walked so far. We'd better return."

As they started toward the clinic, Hildy's thoughts jumped, and she frowned.

Spud caught the expression. "What're you thinking?"

"Oh, it'll wait," she said evasively. Because of Ben's health problems, Hildy didn't feel it was the right time to say anything about asking Mr. Farnham if he could give her father a job.

"Must be something besides Ben's health," Spud guessed.

Hildy's face tightened and her voice took on a sad tone. "Daddy says we're moving to Flatsville."

Spud stopped abruptly. "What?"

Hildy explained as briefly as possible, trying to keep her voice from breaking.

When she had finished, Spud took a long, shuddering breath and slowly blew it out. She waited for him to comment, but he started walking in silence.

Alarmed, Hildy asked, "Well, aren't you going to say anything?"

Again, he didn't answer, but kept walking.

"Say something!" Hildy cried, stepping in front of him.

He looked into her eyes with such a soft, tender expression that her heart leaped into her throat and seemed to catch there.

"Hildy, I never met anyone in my whole life who was as good to me as you are," he said slowly. "If it hadn't been for you, I might still be hoboing around the country. Sooner or later, I'd probably have fallen under the wheels of a freight train or been knifed by some other 'bo who didn't like me for one reason or another. Hildy, I probably owe you my life."

"Oh, Spud!" she whispered, touched by his words.

He gripped her hands with sudden intensity. "Do you want to move away, Hildy?"

"Of course not! I want to stay here, forever!"

"Then I'll help you find a way," he said, releasing her hands.

Hildy felt hope surge through her body, warming her from the inside. "I'm going to stay in Lone River!" she cried, throwing out her arms in relief. "I don't know how, but I'm going to do it!"

Then the enormity of what she had said hit her. A voice in her brain warned, *There isn't time! Besides, even if there was time, it's too big a job.*

Doubt swept through Hildy like a blast of Arctic wind. Still, she looked at Spud and managed a weak smile. "We'll find a way! We've got to!"

But the terrible doubt seized her heart with an icy grip. She and Spud walked back to the clinic in silence.

CHAPTER
FOUR
—

# A HINT OF THE FUTURE

The next day began the last week of school before Christmas vacation. All morning, Hildy's emotions alternately rose in hope and plunged in despair over Ben's problem and her own. She tried to hold out hope that medical tests on the old ranger would find he did not have terminal lung cancer. She also tried to believe her father would find work in Lone River so the Corrigan family wouldn't have to leave behind all of Hildy's friends just before Christmas.

At noon, Hildy and Ruby hurriedly ate their lunches, then walked the few short blocks to the downtown stores. Neither girl had any Christmas spirit, but Hildy had to complete her shopping.

The cousins moved in thoughtful, glum silence, their coats pulled tightly about them. The fog had lifted off the ground but still hung overhead in a solid cloud, totally obscuring the sun.

Finally Ruby muttered, "I don't feel no better'n ye do, but ye got to say somethin'."

Hildy sighed. "I'm just sick about Brother Ben. I can't imagine he might really be . . . dying." She had to pause before she could say the dreaded word.

Ruby observed matter-of-factly, "Everybody's got to die, an' he's a mighty old man."

Hildy rankled at her cousin's words. "Don't sound so unconcerned!"

"Ye don't hafta bite muh head off!" Ruby flared, her voice rising. "I feel mighty sorry fer Ben too, but I ain't never been as close to him as ye have. So it don't hurt me as much."

"I'm sorry I snapped at you," Hildy said. When her cousin nodded in understanding, Hildy added quietly, "Ben's a wonderful old gentleman, almost like family."

Ruby's voice was softer as she asked, "Did he say how long he's got left?"

"The doctor won't know until after the tests, but he did say Ben would have some time, if it is cancer."

The girls walked in thoughtful silence past several store windows prominently displaying the Blue Eagle of the NRA, proclaiming, "We do our part." This was one of President Roosevelt's "alphabet" agencies created to help ease the lingering Depression.

At Lone River's only five-and-dime store, the girls pushed open the door. It carried a sign proclaiming, "Nothing Over 49 Cents." Except for the owner and one customer, their backs to the cousins, the store was empty. At the rear of the long, narrow building a Victrola played a Christmas carol from a scratchy record.

Ruby asked, "Whatcha gonna buy in here?"

"I have something for everybody in the family except Molly. She'll never replace Mama, of course, but she's been mighty good to us kids. So I'd like to buy her something special with my silver dollar."

As the cousins continued through the store toward the cash register, the lone customer turned and came toward the girls. "Oh, no!" Hildy said under her breath. "It's Pruda! She's back."

Pruda Frowick was an obnoxious, heavyset eighth-grader

with untidy mouse-colored hair. Before she had moved away
from Lone River a few weeks ago, Pruda had never tried to hide
her dislike of the cousins.

"Well, well," she began, "Look who's shopping at the dime
store like the rest of us po' folks."

Hildy's stomach twisted at the girl's bitter tone, but she managed to control her feelings. "Hi, Pruda," she said. "I thought
you'd moved away."

"We did, but we had to come back to pick up some things
we couldn't get on our old truck the first trip." Pruda hitched
up her black dress, which had obviously been cut down to fit
her stout body. "I heard this morning you're also moving to
Flatsville."

Hildy blinked. "Also?" she asked.

"Sure! Didn't you know that's where we moved? You'n me'll
be in the same school again."

Shooting an anguished glance at Ruby, Hildy asked, "How
do you like Flatsville?"

"Better'n you will! It's full of Okies like me, only I'm proud
of it. You won't fit, seein' as how you got such high-and-mighty
ideas about bein' somebody someday—not to mention them rich
friends you-all got here."

Hildy started to move on, but Pruda continued her attempt
to get on Hildy's nerves. "Now maybe you'll l'arn what this
Depression's really like, 'cause in Flatsville you won't have nobody, includin' that rich banker or that cattleman, Ben Strong."

Hildy tried to step around Pruda, but the belligerent girl
blocked her. "I'll see that you come down off of your high horse
in Flatsville," she threatened.

Ruby's voice took on an ominous tone. "Git outta the way,
Pruda, or I'll snatch ye bald-headed."

The heavy girl glared at Ruby, then stepped aside. As the
cousins passed on down the aisle, Pruda called, "In Flatsville,
you-all won't have nobody to take your side, Hildy Corrigan!
You won't have a friend in the world. Life will be miserable for
you!"

Ruby spun around and took a couple of quick steps toward Pruda. "Ye so much as lay a hand on her, an' ye'll answer to me!"

The girl didn't answer but hurried out of the store. Hildy stared after her. "Oh, Ruby, I can't stand the thought of moving to where she lives! But the only chance I've got is to see if Mr. Farnham will hire Daddy."

"When ye gonna see Mr. Farnham?"

"I don't know."

"Reckon he'll be at his bank now?"

Hildy brightened. "He might. It's only a couple of blocks away. Let's run over and see."

"Go on by yorese'f. I'm a-gonna look around here."

Hildy started to protest, then guessed that Ruby probably wanted to buy a present for her. Hildy nodded and hurried out into the cold, damp fog.

As Hildy reached the bank door that opened onto the corner of the street, she caught a glimpse of Mr. Farnham a block away. *He must be going to lunch,* she decided, breaking into a run. Then she remembered there was only one small cafe in that direction. *I'll cut through the alley and get there just about when he does.*

Hildy ducked into the alley between rows of ancient red-brick buildings, and started to walk around a stack of cardboard boxes that had apparently been dumped outside for burning later. One bright red box caught her eye. She stopped and picked it up. It was about six inches square and in near-perfect condition, except for one slightly crumpled corner. Hildy stopped and examined the box. It was clean inside.

*Maybe I could wrap Molly's gift in it,* she thought, gently straightening out the bent corner. She continued down the alley, carrying the box.

At the far end, a man entered the alley and glanced around. He hesitated at seeing the lone girl, then continued toward her. Hildy stopped in surprise. *Zane!*

She was tempted to run, but instead, she turned to face the back door of a shop. She reached out for the handle as though about to enter. If the leader of the cattle rustlers gave any sign of recognition, she would dash through the shop and escape to the street.

But the beefy man paused at another alley door nearer the street he had come from, then disappeared inside a building.

Hildy debated about what to do. Zane hadn't gotten a good look at her when he and the other two rustlers were stealing the old ranger's livestock. However, at the accident near the clinic, Zane had threatened her and the driver of the car. Zane would surely recognize her now if he saw her up close.

*Still,* she decided, *I've got to see what he's up to.*

Her heart racing with excitement, Hildy cautiously eased down the alley, still carrying the red box.

*Which door did he enter?* she wondered as she neared the end of the alley. All the metal back doors had numbers, but only three had names written on them. Hildy's eyes skimmed each one. *Haberdashery. Bakery. Hardware.* Hildy shook her head. *Which one?*

Suddenly, an unmarked door swung out. Zane reappeared, talking to someone inside. "It's all prime beef," Zane said. "Your customers will be happy."

*Of course! A butcher shop!* Hildy glanced around for a place to hide.

The hardware store's back entry had a small alcove. The girl ducked into its shelter, pressing herself flat against the metal door.

She listened, barely daring to breathe, until she heard Zane's footsteps growing fainter. Very carefully, Hildy peered out from her hiding place.

Zane stood at the far end of the alley. He waved to someone out of sight in the street, then headed back to the butcher shop.

Quickly drawing back, Hildy waited, churning with anxiety. Then she heard a truck in low gear enter the alley. She listened until it stopped and the driver's door opened. Then she slowly peeked again.

*It's the same truck! The right-front fender's still banged up. And those are the same two men, Al and Smokey, that I saw stealing Brother Ben's steers. They must be selling his meat!*

Hildy's mind spun with indecision. *Should I run through the hardware store and tell Mr. Farnham? He could call the police. But then those men will claim it's their beef, and nobody could prove otherwise. If I say those are the same men I saw rustling livestock, it'll be their word against mine. Oh, I wish Ruby were here. Or Spud.*

The boy's words from yesterday leaped into her mind. *"Did you get the license number?"*

"License number!" Hildy breathed aloud. She eased her head out slightly, craning her neck to get a good look at the plates without being seen.

Seconds later she told herself with satisfaction, *I got it!* She tried to fix it in her mind because she had no paper or pencil. Glancing at the pretty red box, she smiled and removed the lid. With her fingernail, she carefully scratched the plate number into the white interior of the box lid.

She closed the lid and glanced up just as Smokey and Al reached into the back of the truck. Each retrieved a side of fresh beef. They carried the meat into the building while the butcher, wearing a bloody apron and paper cuffs up to his elbows, handed Zane some money.

Suddenly the door behind Hildy opened. She spun around. A short, curly-haired man with swarthy skin stood there. He held a small canvas bag marked *Lone River Bank.*

"Hey!" the hardware merchant shouted. "What're you doing here?"

Startled, Hildy stuttered, "I . . . I—"

The merchant angrily interrupted. "I get tired of kids trying to break into my place! I know these are hard times, but that's no reason to steal from me!"

Hildy didn't intend to back away, but the man's loud words made her step into the alley. "I'm not trying to steal anything, mister. Honest! I was—"

"Don't give me that!" he broke in again. "I've had three break-ins since school started. Now you're trying to rob my back room while I work in front of the store. I'm sick of it! And I've caught you red-handed!"

With his free hand, he reached out to seize Hildy's arm, but she twisted away. "Mister, I really wasn't—"

"All right!" The man threw up a hand and started down the alley. "But don't ever let me catch you here again!"

With a sigh of relief, Hildy turned back in time to hear the truck's motor roar to life. The butcher had disappeared inside his shop, and the cattle rustlers' truck began moving toward Hildy.

She saw Smokey standing on the running board of the passenger's side. Zane stood on the other. Suddenly, he pointed to Hildy and shouted at the driver.

*They've recognized me!*

The vehicle hurtled toward her, gaining speed.

# CHAPTER
## FIVE

---

# ANOTHER
# DISAPPOINTMENT

For a moment, Hildy stared in fear as the truck thundered down the alley toward her. Springing to life, she grabbed the handle of the hardware door, but it was locked. She rushed to the next door. *Please, Lord! Let it be open!*

She followed her silent prayer by twisting the knob. It turned. With a sigh of relief, she shoved the door open. The haberdashery storeroom was lined with racks of men's suits. The smell of new clothing and mothballs filled Hildy's nostrils as she slammed the door behind her.

She heard the truck stop outside and the sound of two men at the door. Hildy spun about and raced through the back room, past the startled owner at the cash register, and out the front door.

To her left, she glimpsed the banker as he entered Lone River's only coffee shop, *Betty's Place.* Hildy dashed after him. "Mr. Farnham! Wait!" she called. He didn't seem to hear.

Behind her, Hildy heard a door thrown violently open and Zane's voice. "There she goes!"

She kept running, spurred on by the ominous sound of heavy boots clumping behind her on the sidewalk.

Hildy reached the cafe door, gasping for breath. A man in auto mechanic's coveralls opened the door to step outside. She slipped by him, barely hearing his startled exclamation.

Hildy stopped and glanced around. Except for two ranchers in traditional blue denim, all the other patrons were business-men wearing suits and ties. A skinny man in a white hat and apron served as cook. The only woman in the place was the owner and sole waitress. Betty was slender, with bobbed blonde hair. She turned with the men to stare at Hildy.

The girl spotted the banker as he slid into a chair at an empty table in the far right-hand corner of the cafe. "Mr. Farnham!" Hildy cried, rapidly weaving her way past other chairs and tables. "Mr. Farnham!"

The banker glanced up in obvious astonishment, peering at her over the top of oblong-shaped, silver-framed bifocals. As always, he was well-dressed in a three-piece suit, his heavy gold watch chain stretched across his blue serge vest. "Hildy, what on earth—"

She blurted, "Those men are chasing me!" She pointed to the window. "They're the ones who stole Brother Ben's cattle. And just now I saw them sell some meat to the butcher. I'll bet it's Brother Ben's."

Mr. Farnham looked toward the cafe window just as the two men abandoned their pursuit. The truck careened around the corner and stopped. Zane leaped onto the truck's passenger-side running board and scrambled into the seat. Al followed. The gears grated harshly as the driver shifted into low and ac-celerated down the street.

"I got their license number!" Hildy exclaimed, opening the red box and pointing. "Quick! Call the police! They might catch them before they get away."

"Calm down, Hildy!" the banker urged, reaching up and

gently pulling her into an empty chair beside him. "What's this all about?"

Still panting, Hildy explained, then concluded breathlessly, "Then they saw me and started chasing—"

She broke off as the banker quickly stood and spoke to the owner behind the counter, "Betty, I need to use your phone to call the police."

Hildy sat uncomfortably at the table, aware that patrons were staring at her. She set the red box on the floor beside her chair. In the excitement of being chased, she'd forgotten her original reason for wanting to see Mr. Farnham.

He returned to his seat. "Chief Thorne will be right over. He wants you to wait. I also called Ben Strong. He's on his way here to talk to you, too."

Hildy suddenly stiffened, thinking of the time. "I can't! I've got to get back to school before the final bell rings."

"If you're late, I'll explain to the principal. I'm sure he'll understand that both men will need to talk to you."

Hildy nodded, remembering why she'd been looking for the banker. "Well, while we wait, I want to talk to you about my father. You see . . ."

She paused as a Model B Ford with a red light at the left front window skidded to a stop at the curb. The only policeman in town, who was also naturally the chief, strode purposefully into the cafe.

He was a tall, well-built, middle-aged man wearing a peaked cap, khaki shirt, and matching pants with a Sam Browne belt and holstered revolver. Hildy had met him before, so she greeted him politely and started to tell what had happened.

The chief stopped her. "Let's go outside so the rest of these folks can finish their lunch in peace."

Hildy and the banker followed the officer outside. Some patrons stood by the window, obviously displeased at not being able to hear every last detail of what the girl had to say.

Chief Thorne placed his left foot on the running board of his car. He laid a notebook on his bent knee and made notes while

Hildy retold her story. She shivered, partly from the excitement and partly from the cold, foggy weather. When she had finished, the officer closed his notebook.

"I'll go interrogate Otto, the butcher. You'd better come with me, Hildy."

She turned to the banker, "Mr. Farnham, before I go, there's something very important I must talk to you about. My daddy—"

Chief Thorne interrupted. "You can go by the bank and talk later, Hildy. Right now, we've got to talk to the butcher. If he has names and an address on those men, we can get on their trail before it gets cold."

Feeling her opportunity slipping away, Hildy tried again. "Mr. Farnham, I—"

This time the banker interrupted. "Come by my office when you and the chief have finished with Otto. I'll be through with lunch by then, and I'll be happy to hear you out, Hildy. Oh, and I'll tell Betty where you'll be so Ben can find you when he arrives."

Hildy felt a mixture of frustration and anxiety when she entered the front door of the butcher shop with Chief Thorne. They walked across the sawdust-covered floor. Otto Schmaltz put his butcher knife on the chopping block with some meat he'd been cutting. He smiled, coming toward his visitors, wiping his hands on a towel hanging at the end of the high glass counter.

"Otto," the officer began, clearing his throat, "Hildy here says she saw three men delivering some meat to your back door awhile ago. Is that right?"

The butcher nodded. He was a big man, solidly built with curly graying hair. "Sure. Happens all the time. Ranchers kill a few head of their stock, keep some meat for themselves, and sell me the rest for spending money. Why? Is there a problem?"

"Could be," the chief admitted. "Hildy, tell him what you told me."

She rushed through the whole story, keenly aware that it was time to head back to school, yet knowing she must first talk to the banker about a job for her father.

Otto heard her out in silence. Then he adjusted the pale pink cuffs he made every morning of butcher paper torn from the roll on the high, white countertop.

"I'm sorry if I bought some of Ben's beef, but I had no reason to suspect it was stolen. Those men said it was from their own herds, and I had no reason to doubt them. After all, I buy meat this way all the time."

The chief asked, "Did you know those men?"

"Never saw them before, Chief."

"Did they mention their names or give an address?"

"No, but I didn't see any reason to ask. I examined the meat and saw that it was good. The price was right, too. Sorry I can't be more help."

The chief thanked the butcher and drove Hildy to the bank. At the curb, she slid out of the car and started across the sidewalk toward the bank's big double doors. *I sure hope Mr. Farnham's got a job for my daddy!*

She stopped and looked down the street at the familiar sound of Ben Strong's Packard. Hildy waited as he nosed into the curb and got out of the car.

"I drove into town as soon as I got Matt's call," he began in his soft drawl. "Betty told me where you'd be. I understand you've had some excitement."

Hildy nodded. "Could we sit in your car where it's warm while I tell you about it?" she asked.

When they were seated, Hildy realized it wasn't much warmer under the canvas top than outside on the sidewalk. But at least the dampness didn't seep through her clothes and into her bones. She hurriedly recounted her experiences of the last hour. She concluded, "I've got to ask Mr. Farnham if he has a job for my father."

"I understand," the old ranger assured her. "But the chief told me on the phone that you got that truck's license number. Is that right?"

Hildy nodded, then stiffened, glancing down at her empty

hands. "I scratched the number with my fingernail on the inside of a box lid, but I forgot it at *Betty's Place* when the chief took me to the butcher shop!"

"We'll go get it," Ben replied, starting the car.

The coffee shop was empty, except for Betty. She smiled a welcome to Ben as Hildy ran to the table where she'd left the box on the floor. It wasn't there.

Turning to Betty, Hildy asked anxiously, "Did you find a red box I left in here awhile ago?"

"No, I didn't, honey. But maybe the cook did when he swept up. He's taken all the trash over to his house to burn."

Ben said, "I know where he lives."

Hildy and Ben hurried to the Packard and drove two blocks along streets lined with winter-bare sycamore trees. Smoke curling up from the cook's back yard caused Hildy's heart to sink.

She ran around the small white-frame house and saw at a glance that flames were dying out in the rusted metal drum. Nothing remained.

With anguished eyes, Hildy turned to look up at the old ranger. He put his arms around her and said soothingly, "There, there. Don't take it so hard. We've lost the license number, but I'll find another way to catch up to those rustlers."

Hildy wanted to explain that more than a license number had been lost. So had a pretty box that would have made one of her small gifts look better when her stepmother opened it on Christmas morning. But Hildy mutely followed Ben back to his car. He drove her to the bank, saying he'd wait and then drive her to school after she talked with Matt.

The banker opened the door to his inner office and motioned Hildy to a seat. She was so anxious to talk to him that she barely noticed the rich furnishings. "Mr. Farnham," she began, leaning forward in her chair and looking across the desk at him, "I hate to ask you, but I've got nobody else who can help."

Breathlessly, she explained about her father losing his job and his plans to move to Flatsville. The banker listened politely until she came to her request.

"Mr. Farnham, if you could find a job for my daddy on one of your ranches, he'd work mighty hard. I know he would, and you'd never be sorry you hired him."

The banker leaned across the desk and peered over the top of his glasses. "Hildy, I know your father's a top rider, a fine, all-around hand, and as honest and hardworking as a man can be. But I have a bunch of fine cowboys working for me now. They are all family men, and none of them plans to quit, so far as I know. I'm sure you can understand that I couldn't let one of them go without hurting their families."

Hildy nodded dumbly, feeling her chances for staying in Lone River sinking like a stone in a pond. Her head sagged forward so she was looking unseeingly at the carpeted floor.

The banker stood and walked around the desk. "I'm sorry, Hildy," he said in a low, sincere voice.

"Me too," she replied, rising quickly and almost stumbling from the room.

*There goes my last hope!*

The sickening thought followed her outside to the sidewalk and the dismal fog.

# Chapter Six

# A DANGEROUS ENEMY

The old ranger had waited, as he had promised. Hildy silently slid into the front seat beside him, and he headed the big Packard down the street toward school.

He said sympathetically, "I can see by your face that you got bad news from Matt, Hildy. I'm sorry."

Hildy felt miserable. "Things sure look dark."

"Have you prayed about this?"

"All the time."

"Have you asked God what His will is?"

Hildy thrust her chin out. "No, because I'm sure He'd want us to stay here."

As he slowed the big car in front of the school, the old ranger said softly, "Sometimes what we want and what God wants for us are different. The Scripture says that God's thoughts are higher than ours. But we don't always accept that, especially when we want something so much."

Hildy didn't want to hear that. *I know what's right!* she told herself fiercely. *To stay in Lone River!*

The old ranger seemed to sense her feelings. He changed the

subject. "On Saturday, if this weather improves, I'm going to take Buster up to Quint Armstrong's place in the high country. He's the friend I've told you about. Spud's coming, but it'd be nice to have an extra pair of hands. So would you like to come? Bring Ruby too."

Hildy's interest stirred at the mention of Spud going along. "I'll ask my folks," she said.

That night, after all four younger sisters and their baby brother had gone to bed, Hildy approached her father. He sat on a homemade bench reading a dime Western. His wife sat across from him, darning socks. Hildy repeated her conversation with Ben Strong.

Joe Corrigan said, "Ben doesn't need your help to move that old horse."

Molly removed a sock from the darning egg and spoke quickly. "Joe, I think he invited the kids for other reasons. Ben's not well, and he's all alone. He's especially fond of Hildy."

Hildy shot an appreciative glance at her stepmother. It was this understanding nature that made Hildy want to buy Molly a special Christmas gift.

Joe looked thoughtfully at his daughter. A hint of a smile showed on his lips. "Seems to me that maybe you'd like to go because Spud's going to be there."

"Oh, Daddy! Spud's just a friend."

"So I've noticed," he replied in a teasing tone.

Hildy squirmed, her eyes lowered. "May I go?"

"Yes, if the fog lifts so it's safe to drive."

"Thanks, Daddy." Hildy reached across the table and gave his work-hardened hand a quick squeeze. She started to rise, but he pulled her back down.

"Hildy, you're old enough to know grown-up things, so you may as well hear this. We've got some beans and flour left to eat on for a while, but we're almost out of wood for the stove, and there's no money to buy more."

Hildy knew that their small rented shack would be unbearable without heat. That was especially true now that the cold, dripping fog seemed to hang on forever. Every one of the kids had suffered with colds and coughs, even in the heated house.

Hildy tried to keep her voice calm. "What'll we do?"

"I've heard that almond hulls and walnut shells will burn," he replied slowly. "There's an almond huller business on a ranch outside of town. I'll go there tomorrow and see if I can trade some work for hulls."

Molly asked quietly, "And if you can't, Joe?"

He didn't answer for a moment, staring into the flickering flame of the lamp. Finally he said softly, "I'll have to borrow some money to buy the hulls."

For the first time, Hildy sensed how critical the family's situation was becoming. Hildy knew how much her father hated debt. She asked, "How much do you need?"

He glanced at his wife, his Adam's apple bobbing as he answered without looking at Hildy. "A dollar ought to do it."

It took a moment for her to realize what a difficult thing he had just said. Indirectly, he was asking to borrow from his own daughter.

In that moment, Hildy understood why her father was going to take the only job he could get, even if it meant moving to a terrible place like Flatsville.

She knew that if she loaned her dollar, it couldn't be repaid until after her father was paid at his new place of work. That would be long after Christmas. There would be no money for Molly's gift.

Wordlessly, Hildy got up and quietly entered her bedroom. She heard her sleeping sister's gentle breathing in the unheated room. It was so cramped there was barely space for the two army cots and a couple of lug boxes that served as both dressers and drawers.

Retrieving the Bull Durham sack from under her pillow, Hildy returned to the table. Not a word had been said since her father's mention of borrowing a dollar.

Pulling the drawstring open, Hildy fished with two fingers into the tiny sack that still smelled of tobacco. "Here," she said, extending the coin to him.

Slowly, without meeting her eyes, he took it. "Thanks," he said in a low, husky tone.

Hildy sensed some of his anguish that this painful moment had brought him.

"I love you, Daddy," Hildy said, giving him a quick kiss on the cheek. "I'm going to bed. Good-night."

Hildy hurriedly undressed in the darkness and shivered as she slid under the heavy blankets. She blew her breath into the pillow. When it was warm, she laid her head on it and looked at the darkened ceiling.

Feeling weepy, she folded her hands under the covers and prayed silently. *Lord, my daddy needs a job real soon. But please let him find it around here so we don't have to move away.*

She paused, then added, *Daddy needed my dollar, but now what am I going to do about Molly's gift?*

———————

Hildy posed the question to Ruby the next morning as the ancient red school bus crept through the persistent fog.

Ruby thought for a moment before answering Hildy's question. Finally she said, "Maybe I could ask muh daddy if'n he'd he'p out."

"No!" Hildy spoke more sharply than she'd intended. "Nobody must know but you and me. My father's already hurting enough because he had to borrow from me. You're the only person in the world I would tell about this. I just hope I'm not shaming him by telling you."

Ruby nodded thoughtfully. "Maybe Ben'll leave ye somethin' in his will when—"

"Ruby!" Hildy interrupted so loudly that other students sitting in nearby seats turned in surprise. Hildy lowered her voice and leaned close to her cousin. "Don't you ever say such a thing again!"

"Ye don't have to git so het up about it!" Ruby snapped, pulling away. "I'm a-tryin' to he'p."

Hildy's tone softened. "I know. But try to help some other way."

They rode in silence a few minutes before Ruby spoke again. "Hey! Ye reckon they's a reward fer them thar cattle rustlers?"

Hildy considered that a moment before answering. "There might be. I'll ask Brother Ben."

" 'Course, even if they is a reward, that won't do ye no good less'n ye capture 'em. An' that's a mighty tall order." Ruby paused, then added, "Ye got one advantage; ye know more about 'em than anybody else."

Hildy thought about that possibility through the morning classes, but concluded it was unlikely she could help capture the cattle rustlers. Still, she decided it wouldn't do any harm to keep her eyes open. At noon, she suggested to Ruby that they eat their lunches where they could watch traffic on the main street.

Hildy explained, "Since I've seen that cattle rustler's truck in town before, maybe it'll come by again. This time I brought a pencil and paper to write down the license number."

Ruby pried the round lid off of her shiny lunch pail. It had originally held a pound of lard. "Ain't hardly any chance a-tall o' them a-drivin' down this ol' street whilst we'uns air a-watchin'."

"Maybe not," Hildy admitted, opening her identical lunch bucket. "But I can hope."

The girls watched the traffic while they ate. Hildy had two cold biscuits and a hardboiled egg. That reflected the desperate plight of the Corrigan family's finances. Ruby was better off. She had a potato sandwich, which her father could afford. He was now working as pastor of a small church. Though his salary was minimal, at least it was fairly regular.

Between bites of egg, Hildy repeated Brother Ben's suggestion that Ruby ride along when Buster was taken to the mountains on Saturday.

Ruby stuffed the last bite of sandwich in her mouth before answering. "If'n that ol' Spud wasn't a-goin', I wouldn't mind the ride. Muh daddy tells me that jist a few miles up in the hills from here, they's no fog. Jist lots o' sunshine. I'd like to see some o' that a'gin."

Hildy sighed, wishing Ruby would try to get along with Spud. The cousins finished their lunches and closed the lids on their pails. They had watched diligently, but there had been no sign of the cattle rustlers' truck.

Heading back toward the two-story, red-brick school building, Hildy said, "I wish I'd asked when Brother Ben was going to have those tests."

"Yeah, but what if it turns out he's really got cancer? Then ye'd know for shore that he's really dyin'."

Hildy turned when she heard a familiar sound. "There he is! Pulling up to the curb, too. Come on, let's go see if he knows anything for sure."

"Ye better go by yorese'f. I see a gal over thar that I got to talk to."

Hildy ran to the Packard as the old ranger stepped onto the running board. "Morning, Hildy."

"Morning," Hildy replied. "What brings you here at this time of day?" *I hope it's not bad news,* she thought.

"I've just been to the police station, following up on those cattle rustlers." Ben reached into the pocket of his heavy sheepskin jacket. "Look what just came in to the station." He shoved a wanted poster in front of her.

Hildy's eyes inspected the photo. "That's the same man I saw! Zane!"

"Read what it says under the picture."

She skimmed the bold black lettering:

"WANTED FOR MURDER & PRISON ESCAPE! ZANE VERNON . . ."

Hildy stopped reading and looked in surprise at the old ranger. "Zane Vernon? Is that the same man—"

"The very same," Ben interrupted. "The only prisoner who ever escaped from me, and then bushwhacked me!"

"That was a long time ago."

"Twenty years! He escaped again about a month ago, this time from a Texas prison where he was serving a life sentence for murder. Now he's back in California, doing what he always did: stealing cattle."

A sudden cold chill swept through Hildy's body. "He knows what I look like," she said softly. "He's seen me, and threatened me! Yesterday he chased me with a truck. Oh, Brother Ben! Do you think he'll come after me?"

"Not if I can help it, Hildy." The old ranger set his jaw grimly. "I never thought I'd get the chance to wipe the stain off my career that he left when he escaped. So I'm going to find him and make a citizen's arrest. This time, he's not going to escape."

"That could be dangerous."

He shrugged. "No more than having cancer."

Hildy gulped. "Did you have those tests?"

He nodded slowly. "Doc says I've got a year, maybe eighteen months."

"Oh, Brother Ben!" Hildy whispered, reaching out to take both his hands.

"Doc thinks it was all those cigarettes I smoked for so long before I came back to the Lord that's caused it. Anyway, it's made me think on what's important."

"Like erasing the stain Vernon put on your record?"

"That, among other things."

"You could be in danger, too. So if I could help . . ."

"I thought you'd say that. I've been doing some thinking, and I have some ideas about where to start. This afternoon I'm going to drive into the country to check out my idea. You want to ride along?"

Hildy nodded. "If my folks say it's okay."

"I'll ask them for you and be back after school with their answer. I'll ask Ruby's father if she can come along, too."

As the Packard pulled away, heading west, Hildy started to turn back toward the schoolhouse. Then she glanced to the east and did a double take. A stake-sided truck approached with the right front fender missing. Hildy peered through the dusty windshield.

*That's the same truck! And that's Zane driving!*

Hildy ducked behind the wide trunk of the nearest sycamore tree. She glanced hopefully down the street to see if Brother Ben's Packard was still in sight. It wasn't. Hildy whirled back to watch the truck.

*I'll get the license number when he gets closer.*

Hildy quickly set her lunch pail on the ground and fished pencil and paper from her coat pocket. In her excitement, she dropped the pencil. Stooping quickly, she retrieved it, taking her eyes off the truck. When she straightened up, the truck had passed and was turning left onto Maple Street across from the school.

Hildy strained to see the rear plate, but it was covered with mud. She groaned as the vehicle proceeded down the side street, lined with elms. Then the truck slowed. It eased toward the curb at the end of the block.

*He's stopping!*

Frightened but alert, Hildy watched the cattle rustler jump down from the truck's cab. He hurried toward a house set well back off the street.

*I have to get that license number again!*

Making sure no cars were coming, she dashed across the street. She stayed on the sidewalk opposite the parked truck and cautiously walked forward.

She ignored a silent warning inside her brain. *Remember, he's an escaped murderer! He shot Brother Ben, and he knows I'm the only one around here who can recognize him. So watch out! If he sees me . . .*

Hildy shook off the fearful thoughts. Carefully, she slipped closer and closer to the parked truck. She concentrated so hard that she forgot to watch for the driver.

CHAPTER
SEVEN

——

# THE PRINCIPAL'S OFFICE

With pounding heart, Hildy reached the far end of the quiet north-south Maple Street across from the parked truck. She eased behind the last cluster of elm trees, pencil and paper ready to write the truck's front license plate number.

Yesterday, just before she had been chased by the three cattle rustlers in that truck, the numbers had been easy to read. Now both front and rear plates were obscured by red mud.

*Got to get closer,* she told herself.

She glanced nervously around. Nobody was in sight. Maple Street was so still that she could hear the droplets of dense fog as they fell from the overhead tree branches and splattered on her coat collar.

Tense as a cat about to spring, she cautiously moved to where she could make out the first part of the license number. She hastily scribbled it on her paper, then placed the pencil between her lips. With her free right hand, she started to brush the mud off the last numbers on the plate. Her coat restricted her movement. Quickly unbuttoning it, she again bent and started rubbing the license plate.

"What are you doing?"

The man's voice behind her made Hildy jump in surprise. The pencil fell from her open mouth. She whirled around, her heart leaping into a wild gallop.

Zane Vernon stood three feet away, his eyes bright with suspicion. Then he frowned and leaned toward her. "Oh, it's you again! What's going on?"

"Uh . . ." Hildy tried to think of something to say, but couldn't. She started backing away slowly.

"No, you don't!" His right hand shot out and gripped her left forearm inside the coat sleeve. Her paper fluttered to the sidewalk. "Who are you?" he demanded, his voice rough and harsh. "What are you doing?"

Hildy jerked her arm back, but the man's grip was firm. "Let me go!" she demanded, struggling harder.

"Not until you answer my questions!" There was an angry glint in Vernon's cold blue eyes. "I'm tired of you watching me! What's your name?"

"Uh . . . Hildy." Her voice was low.

"Hildy who? Speak up, girl!" Vernon gave her arm a severe jerk, making her head snap.

"Hildy . . ." she hesitated, trying again to pull her arm free. She felt it slip slightly inside the coat sleeve. With sudden hope, she quickly stepped toward him.

The surprise motion caused Vernon to loosen his grip. Instantly, Hildy pulled her hand free. The man's grip tightened on the coat sleeve, but Hildy slid her arm out of it.

She spun away, leaving the coat in his hands. She fled in panic toward the school.

"Stop! Come back here!" Vernon's angry command followed Hildy, lending speed to her fleeing feet.

She heard him start after her, his boots clopping loudly on the concrete sidewalk.

*O Lord!* Hildy's silent prayer shot out as she neared the east-west main street. She briefly looked both ways prior to crossing, hoping there were no cars coming. She groaned at the sight of two coming from opposite directions.

They had slowed in compliance with the school-zone signs, but the cars were still close enough to be a hazard if Hildy dashed across in front of them.

She glanced back. Vernon was gaining fast. Hildy swiveled her head back toward the two cars. *I can beat them across!* She rushed into the marked crosswalk, running with all the speed she could muster.

She leaped onto the curb by the school just as brakes squealed behind her. She risked a look back. The driver of the east-bound car had stopped with his front bumper inches from Vernon's legs. The driver stuck his head out the car window and yelled at the man.

The rustler took a step back from the bumper and looked toward Hildy. "I know where to find you!" he yelled, then spun around and ran toward his truck.

Hildy was still panting when she raced up the steep outside stairs to the school's second floor.

Ruby shoved herself away from the big double glass doors. "Whar ye been? An' whar's yore coat?"

"Tell you inside," Hildy answered, pulling the doors open. The hallway was warm, heated by steam radiators. Hildy leaned weakly against the wall by the principal's office and blurted out her story. She finished with, "Now he knows where to find me because he saw me run to school. He's also got my coat and my paper with part of the license number written on it."

Ruby shook her head till her short blonde hair bounced. "If'n he's as mean as Brother Ben says he is, that thar Zane feller is a-gonna be all riled up. I reckon he ain't gonna sleep easy till he knows what yo're up to."

"I know," Hildy replied with a groan. She paused, frowning. "I wonder who lives in that house where he parked the truck." Hildy's excitement soared. "Hey! Maybe that's a clue that will help us! You and I could walk down there and—"

"Hold it!" Ruby protested. "I ain't a-goin' no place near thar, nor that rustler, if'n I kin he'p it."

The urge was so strong that Hildy thought of another way to get there. "I think Brother Ben would drive me by if I asked him."

"While yo're a-askin', don't fergit to find out how come Zane excaped from Ben, then bushwhacked him. An' how that ol' hoss saved him."

The outer door to the principal's office opened. A tiny wisp of a woman with glasses and graying hair scurried out into the hallway. She stopped short at sight of the cousins.

"Oh, there you are!" she exclaimed. "I was just heading for your classroom to leave a message with your teacher. Mr. Wiley wants to see you, Ruby."

"Me?" Ruby exclaimed. "What fer, Miz Perkins? I ain't done nothin', nary a blessed thing to git sent to the principal's office."

The secretary smiled without humor. "He didn't say, but I suggest you obey immediately." She turned and hurried back into the office.

Ruby turned to Hildy. "I ain't done nothin' a'tall! An' even if'n I had, ye'd be jist as guilty, 'cause we do ever'thing together!"

"Well, since he didn't send for me, it has to be about something else—involving only you. But what?"

"Reckon I'd best go in an see what's up," Ruby said. "See ye back in class."

Hildy watched her cousin head for the wooden door with black lettering on the frosted window: EBENEZER WILEY, PRINCIPAL. Then Hildy headed for her next class.

The fourth and fifth periods passed, but Ruby didn't return. When the bell rang after the fifth period, Hildy dashed down the hallway to the principal's office. Miss Perkins, seated behind a small desk in the outer office, looked surprised when Hildy inquired about Ruby.

"Why, she was in with Mr. Wiley only a few minutes," the secretary explained. "I can't imagine where she's been since then."

Hildy's eyes went to the second, inner office behind Miss Perkins. The solid wooden door was closed, but Hildy could hear Mr. Wiley's voice, apparently he was talking on the phone.

"Was she upset when she left?" Hildy asked.

"If you mean, was she crying, the answer is no. However, I'm sure she was angry. She slammed that door so hard going out that I thought the window would crack."

"Do you know why Mr. Wiley wanted to see her?"

The secretary looked owlishly through her round metal-frame glasses. "I'm afraid that's confidential."

Hildy thanked the woman and reentered the hallway. Most of the students had passed to their sixth and last period of the day, so the corridor was nearly empty. Hildy knew it was almost time for the tardy bell, but she couldn't go to her final class without finding Ruby.

Now really concerned, Hildy ran down the hallway, dodging a few late students heading for their respective classrooms. Hildy hurriedly checked the girls' lavatory, the cloak room, and the nurse's office.

*Zane has never even seen Ruby, so he'd have no reason to grab her,* Hildy told herself. *But maybe I'd better look outside, anyway.*

She dashed to the great double doors that opened onto the outside stairs. Hildy stepped into the damp coldness and shivered.

A quick glance at the silent school grounds showed that Ruby wasn't anywhere in sight. Hildy skipped down the steep stairs to look across the main street and down Maple Street, where Zane had pursued her.

There was no sign of him, his truck, Ruby, or Hildy's coat as the tardy bell for sixth period sounded.

*Daddy's going to be very upset when I come home without my coat,* she warned herself. Hildy did feel a little better about her cousin. *I don't think Zane has her, so I guess whatever Mr. Wiley said to her upset her enough to send her into hiding. But where is she now?*

There was only one other possibility, Hildy decided. She dashed across the school grounds, past the dirt volleyball court and the lower-floor windows that marked the boys' manual-training shop, and on to the bus sheds.

Overhead, the sun showed just a faint hint of trying to break through the perpetual fog. With teeth starting to chatter in spite of her exertion, Hildy darted into the bus sheds.

The smell of grease and dust assaulted her nostrils. She looked briefly around at the work benches, the tools, and the remaining three red buses.

Her eyes fell on the high, narrow bus she and Ruby rode to and from school. It was affectionately called *The Fish Can*. Twice daily, students were packed like sardines into the relic, which had isinglass instead of glass windows along the sides.

The bus door was open, so Hildy stepped up and looked inside. At first, she saw nothing in the darkened interior. She started to leave when she heard a sob.

In seconds, Hildy knelt beside her cousin, who was curled up on the very last seat in the back. "Ruby! Ruby!"

"Go 'way!" Her voice was barely audible. She waved an impatient hand at Hildy without raising her head from where it was cradled on her forearms.

"What's the matter?" Hildy demanded, turning her cousin's face upward. Her eyes were swollen and her nose was red. "What happened?" Hildy cried.

"Oh, Hildy!" Ruby's voice dripped with sadness. She sat up quickly and threw her arms around her cousin. "Ye cain't never guess what turr'ble mean things he said!"

"Who? Mr. Wiley?"

Nodding vigorously, Ruby pulled back and rubbed her nose with the back of her hand. "Uh-huh."

"What did he say?"

"He said . . ." Ruby sniffed and gazed at Hildy with bleary eyes. "He said . . . oh, I cain't say it!"

Hildy gripped her cousin's shoulders hard with both hands. "Say it! Is he expelling you from school?"

"Worse!"

"Tell me!"

Ruby sniffed again. "He done tol' me . . ."

"Hey, you two!" A man's voice made both girls whirl to face the front of the bus. Hildy recognized one of the drivers.

He stood in the open door wiping his hands with a greasy rag. "You girls know you're not supposed to be here. Come on out."

Hildy was about to explode with curiosity over Ruby's problem. But she didn't want to ask more in front of the bus driver. The cousins hurried wordlessly to the concrete sidewalk just as Ben Strong's Packard pulled to the curb.

As the girls turned toward him, he leaned across the seat and quickly rolled down the passenger-side window. "I was going to look for you two," he called excitedly. "Get in! I've got big news!"

# Chapter Eight

# FOLLOWING A CLUE

Hildy slid across the Packard's leather seat, followed by Ruby. Hildy was eager to hear what news the old ranger had, and to tell him about seeing Zane again. But she was also concerned about what had upset Ruby.

Ben reached for the gear shift. "Your fathers gave me permission for you—Ruby! You been crying?"

She rubbed her red nose again with the back of her hand. "I reckon so."

"What happened?" the old ranger asked anxiously.

"It don't rightly matter none," Ruby answered. "What's yore big news?"

"It'll wait," he replied. "Ruby, if I'm butting in where I shouldn't, please forgive me. But I care about you, and if I can help in whatever's making you cry—"

"Ye do?" Ruby interrupted, leaning forward slightly to glance past Hildy to the driver. "Ye shore 'nuf care?"

"Very much," Ben answered.

Hildy urged impatiently, "Tell us, Ruby. What did Mr. Wiley say that upset you so?"

"Well," Ruby began, sniffing loudly. "At fu'st, he hurt muh feelin's somethin' awful; then what he said made me so mad I could've spit nails. I wanted to crawl in a hole an' die. That's when I come out to the bus shed—"

"Ruby!" Hildy broke in impatiently. "What did he say?"

"I'm a-tellin' ye, so hold yore hosses! He done said I was a plumb disgrace on accounta the way I talk. He said I either gotta improve real quick-like, or all muh teachers say I got to be held back another year."

Hildy stared at her cousin. "That's it? That's all he said to make you cut classes and scare me to death trying to find you?"

"Ain't that 'nuf?" Ruby flared. "I done been held back once a'ready. If'n it happens ag'in, I'll turn into a old gray goose afore I git outta grammar school!"

For a second, Hildy was annoyed that Ruby had frightened her. This was followed by a wave of relief. She started giggling.

Ruby snapped, "Why are ye a-laughin' at me?"

Hildy put both arms around her cousin. "I'm not laughing *at* you! I'm just so relieved that you're okay! When I couldn't find you, I thought Zane Vernon had grabbed you."

"Why would he do that?" Ruby demanded indignantly, gently withdrawing from Hildy's hug. "He ain't never seen me, and I ain't seen him neither."

"I know, but my imagination was running wild." Hildy turned to look up at the old ranger. "What's your news?"

Before he could answer, Ruby grumbled, "Ye don't even keer what's a-gonna happen to me now."

"Of course I care!" Hildy turned back to Ruby. "But you can learn to speak properly—"

"No, I cain't!" Ruby broke in hotly. "I never l'arned to talk like other folks, an' I ain't a-gonna!"

"Nobody can force you, of course," Hildy said. "But I wouldn't be surprised if a lot of good things happened to you if you did decide to improve the way you speak."

Ben checked that traffic was clear, then eased the big Packard forward. "Ruby, you're coming into young womanhood. Pretty soon you'll be self-conscious about how you talk."

Ruby asked suspiciously, "Air ye a-makin' out that I cain't l'arn to talk as good as anybody else?"

"On the contrary," Ben answered. "I believe most folks do what they really want to do and make excuses for the rest."

"I kin talk as good as anybody in the whole wide world if'n I want to. Even as good as ol' Spud with his fancy two-dollar words," Ruby muttered sourly.

Ben agreed. "Of course you can—if you want to. That's the secret of most things: wanting something enough."

"That's right," Hildy added, and turned to the old ranger. "Let's hear your news, Brother Ben."

"Okay, but first you should know I talked to your fathers and got permission for you to take a ride with me. We're also going to pick Spud up at his high school."

Ruby groaned. "It ain't bad 'nuf what that mean ol' principal done to me. Now I gotta ride with Spud!"

"You get along with him!" Hildy warned, giving her cousin a hard look. When Ruby lowered her eyes, Hildy looked expectantly back to the old ranger. "And?"

"I talked to the butcher who bought those carcasses from the cattle rustlers, but he couldn't tell me much. So I went by the sheriff's office. That's where I got my news. A cattle rancher had called to say he'd found where some stock had been butchered. One of the fresh hides had my brand."

Hildy asked, "Is that a clue you can use to help find those rustlers?"

"It's possible," Ben replied, turning right onto the main street and driving west in front of the school. "I also learned how Zane Vernon escaped from prison."

Hildy suddenly remembered something. "Is there a reward for him?"

"Nope."

Hildy's shoulders sagged. Her hope of a reward for capturing the escaped convict was gone, and with it, another possibility for not having to move away.

"But I don't need money to go after him," Ben said grimly. "I just want to blot out the stain he put on my law-enforcement record. If I can find him, and make a citizen's arrest, then bring him in, I can die in peace."

"Don't say that!" Hildy replied. "You're going to be all right, Brother Ben."

"Denying it won't help, Hildy," he replied gently.

Hildy had almost forgotten to tell Ben something. She said excitedly, "Brother Ben, I saw Zane again today!" She pointed ahead to Maple Street and quickly explained what had happened. She concluded, "I can remember the first three numbers on the license plate, if that'll help."

"It should," the old ranger replied. "My contacts at law-enforcement agencies can run it through Sacramento and give me an idea of where the owner of that truck lives. Right now, we'll drive by that house for a quick look."

Ben slowed as he drove past the place where Zane had entered earlier. "Seven-o-nine," the old ranger read the house number. "I'll check with the police to find out who lives there. That'll give us another clue to check out. Well, let's pick up Spud and go see that rancher who found the cowhides."

Spud was waiting on the corner by a small grocery store across from the high school. "What's up, Ben?" Spud asked after greeting everyone and sliding into the backseat.

The old ranger explained about the rancher finding a cowhide with Ben's brand and Hildy's experience with seeing Zane Vernon again. "So," Ben concluded, heading the car eastward out of town, "I thought you three might like to help me scout around and see if we can pick up any clues to Vernon's whereabouts now."

Hildy twisted in the front seat to look at Spud, but he was studying Ruby's face in the rearview mirror. "What happened to you?" he asked, lightly touching Ruby's left shoulder.

"None o' yore beeswax!" she snapped, shaking his hand off.

Spud turned questioning eyes to Hildy.

She shrugged. "Maybe she'll tell you later." Hildy looked at Ben. "Where are we going?"

"I had planned to go directly out to where those hides were found and see if we could find any clue that might help us find Vernon. But I've been thinking of something you said, Hildy."

"What's that?"

"You said the mud you rubbed off the license plate was red?"

"Yes, why?"

"Sounds like adobe mud to me, and there's only one place around here where I've seen that kind of soil. That mud had to be splattered on the truck since you saw it yesterday, so that's a fresher clue than the cowhides. We'll look there first and hope we beat the fog coming back down. But we'll stop by my place and get a coat so you won't freeze when we get out of the car."

When the Packard stopped at the old ranger's ranch, Buster ran to the corral fence and whinnied a welcome. Hildy smiled as she followed Ruby out of the front seat.

"I think he missed you, Brother Ben."

"We've been through a lot together," he said, leading the way toward the back porch.

Ruby asked, "Air ye a-gonna tell us how that ol' hoss saved yore life?"

"It hurts to even think about," he answered quietly. "But after we find a coat for Hildy, I guess I can put my shame aside long enough to tell you."

A few minutes later, Hildy walked out of the ranch house wearing one of Ben's coats. It hung below her knees while her head was almost lost in the sheepskin collar. She shoved the sleeves up so that her hands were free, but the moment she lowered her arms the sleeves slid several inches past her hands.

Ruby laughed. "Ye shore air a sight!"

Hildy smiled and moved her arms up and down, making the loose sleeve ends flop around. "I guess I am."

Buster whinnied again, thrusting his head across the top corral rail. Hildy commented, "I hope to ride him again before you take him up to the high country."

"Maybe you can," Ben replied. "But right now we'd better check on that adobe mud before the fog settles down and we can't see anything."

After the Packard reached a deserted dirt road, Ben headed eastward toward the foothills.

Ruby prompted, "Ye was a-gonna tell us about how that thar ol' hoss saved yore life."

The old ranger took a slow, deep breath. His jaw set in a grim line for a moment. "Because of my age, I had been relieved of field work and given a desk assignment until my retirement. I knew about Zane Vernon, of course, because we'd been after him for cattle rustling. Then one day . . ." Ben's voice trailed off.

Hildy glanced sharply at him, ready to urge him to say more. Then she saw his face was starting to pucker, and she had the terrible feeling he was fighting tears.

Hildy quickly looked at Ruby beside her in the front seat, then at Spud leaning forward from the backseat. Neither of them said anything. Hildy turned back and waited as Ben negotiated some sharp curves in the rolling foothills.

"One day," Ben continued, his voice low, "some of my ranger friends were chasing Vernon for rustling cows. His horse threw a shoe, so Vernon left the horse behind and went on foot until he came to . . . to an old man's ranch. The man was in his eighties, a widower. Well, he didn't know that Vernon was a wanted man, so . . . so . . ."

Again, Ben hesitated. Hildy reached out and gently touched him on his right arm. "You don't have to tell us," she said quietly.

The old ranger's Adam's apple bobbed, then he shook his head. "I have to talk about it. So naturally, the old man extended typical western hospitality, as he would to any stranger. Vernon ate the meal he was offered, then announced he needed a horse. The old man said his wasn't for sale. Vernon said he was taking him anyway. When the old man tried to stop him, Vernon . . ."

Hildy distinctly heard Brother Ben's voice break. "Please!" she said gently. "It hurts too much for you to talk about it, so don't—"

"Vernon struck the old man with his gun barrel. Then Vernon stole the horse and rode off. It was two days before anyone came by the old man's place. By then he was dead."

Ben turned to look at Hildy, Ruby, and Spud. "The man Vernon killed was . . . my father."

Hildy saw tears spring to the old ranger's eyes before he could turn away and look straight ahead.

Hildy, Ruby, and Spud exchanged silent glances.

Finally, Ben continued, "My superiors naturally didn't want me to get involved in pursuing Vernon because they said it was too personal. But I wouldn't listen. Even if they'd fired me on the spot, I wouldn't have stopped. I wasn't a Christian in those days, so I wanted to avenge my father. I saddled Buster, who was a young horse then, and started trailing Vernon."

Hildy felt her own eyes grow hot with unshed tears as the old ranger paused, eyes fixed on the dirt road unwinding before them, climbing higher into the hills.

"I rode through thick brush as high as my head for three days," Ben continued. "I guess Vernon figured nobody could follow him through that brush, so he built a small fire. I smelled the smoke, ground-hitched Buster, and snuck ahead on foot. Surprised Vernon frying some hardtack in bacon grease. I had him 'cuffed almost before he knew I was there."

Ben hesitated and sighed softly before continuing. "The next morning, with Vernon on my father's stolen horse and me on Buster, we started back. That's where I made a mistake."

"What happened?" Hildy prompted eagerly.

Ben's tone changed. He pointed through the windshield. "Right around this curve, we'll see where that adobe mud is."

Hildy was anxious to hear the rest of Ben's story, but she looked ahead as the Packard rounded the curve. Then she let out a startled exclamation.

"Look! There's the rustlers' truck! And there they are, too!"

"Now what're we gonna do?" Ruby asked.

# Chapter Nine

# A TALE OF AMBUSH

Hildy tensed as the old ranger's big Packard slowed coming out of the curve. Hildy saw the cattle rustlers' truck parked on a short wooden bridge over a seasonal creek. The three men, apparently having heard the car coming, were scrambling to get back into the cab.

"Quick, Hildy," Ben exclaimed, "scoot down inside that coat as far as you can. They mustn't recognize you."

Hildy instantly obeyed, grateful that the coat she'd borrowed from the old ranger was much too big for her. The high sheepskin collar slid past her face.

Ben continued, "We'll have to pass them. Spud, you and Ruby just act natural. Don't do anything to make them suspicious. Spud, try to get that license number, but don't let them see what you're doing."

From inside the coat, Hildy asked, "What if Zane recognizes you?"

"It's been twenty years since we last saw each other, and that was in another state."

"But you recognized him the other day," Hildy reminded Ben.

"I know, but it'll be harder for Vernon to see me inside this car. Okay, here we go past them."

Hildy held her breath until the Packard had passed and the old ranger breathed a sigh of relief.

He asked, "Did you get the number, Spud?"

"I think so, but that mud made it hard to read."

"Good! Now my law-enforcement contacts will surely be able to tell me who that truck is registered to and where he lives. 'Course, it could be stolen."

Hildy slowly stuck her head out of the coat, like a turtle extending its neck from the shell. "What do you think they were doing out here?"

Ben said, "My guess is that they were disposing of some fresh cowhides in that creek." He glanced in the rearview mirror. "I don't think they're suspicious of us, because they're falling well behind.

"Anyway, finding those men here confirms my suspicions about them returning to this area. That's where the red adobe mud came from that's on the license plate. Now we'll take the next side road and circle back to town. Then I'll call the sheriff's office so they can follow up. I don't want to risk Vernon seeing my car around here again."

When the old ranger turned off, he announced that the truck was completely out of sight. That prompted Ruby to ask Ben if he'd continue telling how Vernon had escaped twenty years ago.

The old ranger's face grew grim. "It was coming onto dusk when I caught Vernon, so I handcuffed him for the night. At first light, I put him on the horse he'd stolen from my father. A prisoner's hands are usually cuffed behind his back, but Vernon was afraid he wouldn't be able to stay in the saddle if a snake or something spooked the horse. I recuffed him in front so he could pull the reins if necessary. Then I mounted Buster and started following Vernon out of the brush. About noon . . ."

As his voice trailed off, Hildy glanced up at Ben. Drops of

perspiration popped out on his forehead and he seemed to be having trouble breathing.

"What's wrong?" Hildy exclaimed in alarm.

Ben slowed and steered toward the shoulder of the dirt road. "I'm having some of those symptoms Doc warned me about: sweats and irregular breathing. I'll stop for a minute. Then I'll be all right."

Hildy wasn't so sure of that. She exchanged anxious glances with Ruby and Spud and guessed they had the same doubts. Hildy looked around the countryside for a ranch house where help might be found, but there was none.

"What can we do?" Hildy asked anxiously, taking the old ranger's right hand where it gripped the steering wheel.

"There's nothing anybody can do," Ben replied weakly, seeming to fight for breath. "Just wait."

It seemed like hours before the old ranger took a deep breath and wiped his brow. "It's passed," he said, starting the car again.

Hildy prayed silently and fervently on the slow trip into town. There, at his young passenger's insistence, Ben drove directly to the medical clinic. There Spud telephoned Matt Farnham.

Darkness and the dense fog had settled heavily over Lone River before the banker arrived. Doc Carter assured Hildy, Ruby, and Spud that he would keep Ben overnight for observation. There was nothing more to be done for him, so Matt Farnham drove Ruby home first, then Hildy.

Hildy quieted her family's fears over being so late by explaining all that had happened that day. She concluded, "I'm sure Ben will be all right."

When everyone had asked enough questions to satisfy them, their father led the whole family into the kitchen. He showed a galvanized bucket full of the almond hulls he'd bought with the dollar he'd borrowed from Hildy.

"They burn hot," he explained, "but the first time I threw some into the stove, I nearly smothered the fire. Took awhile for it to burn through. So we have to remember not to put in too many hulls at a time."

Hildy was glad that the family would have heat, yet she felt uneasy because Christmas was coming fast, and she had no way of buying a special gift for Molly.

Hildy's father seemed to sense her concern. He instructed the younger children to stay in the kitchen with their step-mother. He asked Hildy to come with him into the living room. He closed the door to the kitchen and seated himself at the homemade table.

Hildy yielded to his invitation to sit on the bench across from him. He reached across the cracked oilcloth cover and turned down the kerosene lamp, which had started to smoke the glass chimney.

"Hildy," he began, "because you're the oldest, and are already helping us in this hard time, Molly and I want you to know that I'm going to sell the Rickenbacker."

Hildy was surprised. She knew that the big car was the only thing her proud father had to show the world that he was getting by in hard times. "Why, Daddy?"

"I've got to have another car to get to and from work in Flatsville. So I'm planning to trade the Rickenbacker to someone who has a smaller car. Then I'm hoping to get a little cash to boot."

He hesitated, then added in a low, sad tone, "We need the cash to buy beans and flour and such things."

Hildy squirmed uncomfortably, her mind racing with guilty thoughts. *I should have known. Since he's not working, he not only had to borrow my dollar to buy almond hulls, but now he's got to find money to feed us.*

"So," he continued, "I heard about a fellow in Flatsville who wants a big car like mine. He's got a couple of smaller cars to trade: a Chevy and a Star. If I'm any good as a horse trader, we'll come home with a smaller car and some cash besides."

Hildy blinked in surprise. "We?"

"I want you to come along this Saturday."

"Oh, Daddy, I can't do that! Remember? That's when I'm supposed to go with Brother Ben to take his horse up to his friend's place in the mountains."

"From what you told me, he's probably not going to be well enough to go anywhere this weekend."

"He's going to be all right!" Hildy exclaimed.

Her father reached across the table and took her hands in his. "No, he's not. You've got to face that, Hildy, just as you've faced other things in life, like your mother dying, and the fact this Christmas is probably going to be the worst one of your life."

Hildy felt a surge of anger start deep within her. She wasn't sure if it was from knowing that her father was right about Brother Ben, or because she couldn't go with him to take Buster to the mountains. Or maybe it was because she hated moving away.

"Daddy," she said, fighting to keep her voice under control, "I don't want to go to Flatsville—now, or ever."

She saw his jaw muscles twitch. "I don't want to go either." His voice took on a hard edge. "But sometimes we don't get what we want in life. You've got to accept this: we're moving to Flatsville before Christmas."

In frustration, Hildy leaped up, making the lamp rock. "Daddy, I can't do it!" She turned and rushed into her bedroom, her whole insides ablaze with the intensity of her hurt.

———

The next morning, Hildy awoke with a dull ache and two thoughts: *I wonder how Brother Ben is?* and *I wish there were some way to keep from moving away from here!*

On the bus ride into Lone River through the persistent fog, Hildy wanted to talk about these concerns with her cousin, but Ruby was deep in her own problems.

"I can't make up muh mind what to do, Hildy," she confided in a low voice that nobody else on the noisy bus could hear. "If'n I give in to Mr. Wiley an' all them teachers, they'll let me pass to the 7-A class in January. But I'm used to muh way o' talkin, an' I don't like nobody tellin' me what to do."

"If you're asking my opinion, I'd say to do what I did: lose all trace of colloquialism."

"Don't ye go a-usin' fancy words like ol' Spud!"

"I learned that word from Spud, but I had decided to lose my accent and learn to speak properly long before I met him. You can too, if you want."

"I don't want, so there!"

Hildy didn't feel in the mood to pursue the subject further. "Suit yourself," she said, and let her mind drift back to her concern about Ben's health and trying to think of ways to keep from moving away from Lone River. At noon, she decided she'd run over to the clinic and check on Ben.

At school Hildy and Ruby walked in thoughtful silence down the noisy hallway, each lost in her own problems. As they passed the principal's office with their lunch pails, the door opened and a boy stepped out.

He was neatly dressed in new, yellow corduroy pants and white shirt sleeves rolled up above his elbows. His dark hair had been neatly combed straight back.

The boy looked around uncertainly, then spoke to the cousins as they passed. "Excuse me, but could you show me the way to the homeroom for 7-B?"

Hildy smiled in greeting, glad for a way to ease the tension with Ruby. "That's our class. Come with us."

"Thanks! I'm Glenn Masters. This is my first day."

He was taller than any boy in her class, Hildy decided as she introduced herself and Ruby. He was nice-looking too, Hildy thought, but not as nice as Spud.

Glenn fell into step beside Ruby, glancing down at her with obvious approval. "We moved here from Fresno. You lived here a long time?"

Hildy, aware that the question was really directed to her cousin, waited for her to answer. When she didn't, Hildy glanced at Ruby and saw a slight red flush on her cheeks. Hildy blinked with surprise and looked again.

The first bell rang noisily, giving Hildy a moment to look

closely at her strangely silent cousin.

Ruby's hazel eyes were trying to look straight ahead, down the hallway full of jostling students, but Hildy saw Ruby stealing glances at the new boy.

When the bell had fallen silent and Ruby still hadn't replied to Glenn's question, Hildy said, "No, we both came here from the Ozarks last summer."

The boy stopped in surprise. "You did? So did I—well, originally, that is. My folks have been in California a couple of years now." He paused, then asked, "How come you don't have an accent?"

Hildy parried, "Why don't you?"

Glenn grinned, and Hildy realized one corner of his mouth went up slightly higher than the other. "I got tired of being called an 'Okie' and 'Arky,' so . . ." He shrugged, then concluded, "I worked on losing my accent."

Ruby finally found her voice. "Yonder's our class."

Glenn looked down at her and grinned. "I've practiced so hard I can't do that anymore."

Ruby frowned. "Cain't do what no more?"

"Talk the way I used to."

Hildy saw Ruby's face tighten. A sudden flicker of anger showed in her eyes as she looked up at the tall boy. "Air ye a-sayin' I talk funny?"

Hildy shook her head in warning to Glenn. He caught the look. "Uh . . ." he said, glancing hurriedly away. "No, of course not. Excuse me, I think I recognize a kid I used to know in Fresno. I'll see you girls later."

Hildy studied her cousin's face as the new boy hurried away. Ruby's chin seemed to quiver a moment.

"We didn't need him a-hangin' around, nohow," she grumbled.

Hildy asked in surprise, "Are you starting to notice boys?"

"Didn't hardly notice him a-tall," Ruby protested as the tardy bell started to ring. Both girls dashed from the cloakroom into the classroom and took their seats. A moment later, Glenn entered and approached the teacher. Hildy looked at Ruby and watched as she pretended not to notice, but she stole a sly glance at the boy.

Hildy smiled to herself, then shook her head. *Too bad! They seemed to take an instant liking to each other, but the moment she opened her mouth, he ran like a scared rabbit. Maybe I can talk to her about that at lunch.*

When the bell rang at noon, the cousins retrieved their lunch pails and coats from the cloakroom and headed outside. It was still foggy and cold.

"Let's walk over to check on Brother Ben," Hildy suggested. "I'm really concerned about him. And I want to talk to you about what happened with that new boy."

"I don't want to hear another word about him!" Ruby snapped. "He puts me in mind o' Spud and his highfalutin ways. Oh, look! Yonder comes Ben now!"

# CHAPTER
## TEN
---

# A MISERABLE TOWN

With a glad cry, Hildy ran to meet the old ranger as he eased the big Packard to the curb. Ruby followed at a slower pace.

Hildy stuck her head through the open passenger-side window. "Brother Ben, how're you feeling?"

"Fine, thanks."

"Ruby and I were going to run over to the clinic in a couple of minutes to check on you."

"Doc let me go early this morning. He said I just had a little spell, but it passed, and I'll be fine as long as I don't overdo it."

"You take care of yourself," Hildy urged.

"Yeah," Ruby said, coming up and sticking her head in the window beside her cousin's. "We'uns air plumb used to havin' ye around."

"Thanks," Ben replied in a soft tone. "I like being around too." His voice changed. "Oh, Hildy, I stopped in at Betty's for breakfast, and she gave me something that belongs to you."

He reached onto the floorboards in front of the passenger's seat and straightened up.

"My box!" Hildy exclaimed, reaching out to take it. "I thought it had been burned."

"Betty thought so, too. Then a customer found it on a shelf in the bathroom. Apparently somebody put it there after you left it in the cafe."

"Oh, thank you!" Hildy quickly removed the lid. "See?" She held it up for him. "There's the license number of the truck that I scratched in with my fingernail."

"Yes. I took the liberty of opening it at Betty's to make sure it was really the box you'd described to me. Then I went directly to the police station, and they phoned the license bureau in Sacramento. Turns out the truck was stolen near Timber Meadows."

"Isn't that near where your friend lives?" Hildy asked. "The one where you're going to take Buster?"

Ben nodded. "Quint Armstrong. But there was something strange about that truck. After the Lone River police heard back from Sacramento, they phoned the authorities at Timber Meadows. There had been no report of the truck being stolen, so they sent an officer out to the owner's house—fellow name of Jessup. He said he hadn't reported it stolen because he'd been out of town."

"What's so strange about that?" Ruby asked.

Ben shrugged. "Just what we used to call a ranger's hunch. I wonder if maybe the truck wasn't stolen at all, and the owner just said that when he was questioned."

"I don't understand," Hildy admitted.

"I'm not sure I do, either," the old ranger replied. "But the owner's story as he told it to the authorities didn't quite ring true. For example, why would Vernon have escaped from a Texas prison and taken a northern route through Reno into California? That's too long."

Hildy brightened. "Are you thinking that this man who owned the truck and Vernon are together in the cattle rustling business?"

Ben let out a deep breath. "Maybe I'm just too suspicious,

but when we take Buster up to Quint's, I'm going to check out my hunch. You never know where a clue's going to turn up that may help me trap Vernon."

"That reminds me," Hildy said. "Daddy wants me to go with him to Flatsville this Saturday. I'd rather go with you, but I can't."

"I may have to postpone the trip. I heard on the radio this morning that a storm's coming. It'll snow in the mountains but rain down here. That'll get rid of this fog for a while."

"I sure hope so! I'm sick of this fog, and I sure want to go with you and Buster to the mountains."

Ben changed the subject. "What're you going to do with an empty box, Hildy?"

She hesitated, not wanting to say that she would not be able to buy Molly a gift to put in the box, because her father had borrowed her dollar. "I don't know just yet," she answered. "But I'll save it. Might come in handy."

That afternoon when she got home, Hildy slipped out to the barn and hid the red box on a high rafter. *There! It's out of reach of my little sisters.*

The next morning, Hildy awakened to the sound of wind rattling the lone window in her small bedroom. The pane was cracked, so a piece of cardboard had been nailed across the window to help keep out the cold. Hildy pulled back one corner of the cardboard.

"It's clear," she announced, turning at the sound of Elizabeth awakening in her army cot. "That terrible fog's gone. It's going to be a nice day for a change."

The sunshine cheered Hildy as she hurried off to catch the bus, hoping Ruby felt better, too.

"That ol' Glenn thinks he's so dadblamed uppity!" Ruby fumed, slumping down in her seat. "Reckon he's mighty near's bad as Spud."

"Did you notice that when Glenn smiles, one corner of his mouth turns up?"

Ruby's face showed the faintest trace of a smile. "Yeah," she said softly, then frowned. "But that don't mean nothin' to me!"

"Don't you think he's sort of cute?"

Ruby snorted. "Wouldn't make me no never-mind if'n he was the cutest boy ever come down the pike! Let's talk about somethin' else."

During homeroom that morning, Hildy noticed her cousin stealing shy glances at the new boy. But he seemed not to notice her at all.

At noon, Hildy said, "I have a hunch that you and Glenn could be friends if you tried speaking better."

Ruby snapped, "Thar ye go, tryin' to make out I could l'arn to speak diff'rent if'n I wanted! Well, I don't, and I won't, so don't talk about it no more!"

The beautiful crisp, clean weather lasted through the next afternoon. Then it began to warm up as gray clouds, driven by high-altitude winds, scudded across the sky. Rain began Friday night and continued until dawn.

When Hildy's father gruffly awakened her for the trip to Flatsville, he announced that the sky was clearing. That meant the warmer temperature and the wet ground would cause dense fog to return by night. He wanted to go and get back before that happened.

Hildy reluctantly settled back for the drive to Flatsville. She looked sadly around the Rickenbacker, knowing how much her father liked the sedan and how much it must hurt him to trade it off.

They drove in strained silence to the outskirts of Flatsville. It was a dreary stretch of flat, open land without trees or any other attractive features. Hildy glumly viewed countless tar-paper shacks and some tents haphazardly erected along muddy streets.

Hildy took in the traffic going and coming along the main highway through Flatsville. There was a common denominator of defeat about both the people and their vehicles, Hildy noticed.

Each car or truck had out-of-state license plates, mostly from the Dust Bowl areas of Kansas, Texas, and Oklahoma. Every vehicle was old, run-down, and nearly useless. But if it still ran, it moved slowly past, taking despairing people on a vain search for hope.

There was invariably a mattress or two on the roof of passing cars. That reminded Hildy of a common saying: *How can you tell a rich Okie from a poor one? A rich one has two mattresses on the roof.*

All the cars had countless items sticking up from the running boards or tied to the sides. The items ranged from washtubs and butter churns to skillets and cardboard suitcases.

The adults inside the cars had long, skinny faces. Most were economic refugees vainly fleeing the Depression. Some had been farmers driven from their land by deputies with shotguns when banks foreclosed. Others had fled when the drifting sand blotted out the sun, filled their teeth and nostrils with grit, and buried their land. They joined millions of others who were rootless, hungry, and unemployed.

The unshaven men wore faded and patched overalls. The women's cheeks were deeply lined under the projecting front brim of their poke bonnets. The children had uncombed hair and smudges on their thin, pinched faces. Their eyes stared vacantly from sunken sockets.

Hildy moaned in disappointment. "Oh, Daddy, what a terrible place to live!"

"You've never made such a fuss before about where we lived," he said with a touch of anger. "What makes this place different?"

Hildy's strong-willed temperament made her answer with some feeling. "What makes this place different? Do you think it's the terrible things we're seeing and the awful reputation of Flatsville?" She shook her head. "No, Daddy, it's not just that. For the first time in my life, I felt like we were making progress toward getting our 'forever' home. In Lone River, I was beginning to feel like somebody, with friends and roots and a hope for the future. Now we're being forced backward, and that hurts! And it makes me angry."

The moment she finished Hildy felt sorry for her outburst, but she had spoken the truth.

"I understand how you feel, Hildy," her father said quietly, slowing to turn into a garage with a sign that read *Cheap Used Cars*. "But you'll have to accept it. Now, you sit tight while I do a little trading."

While her father haggled with the garage owner, Hildy sat thinking in the front seat of the Rickenbacker. *What am I going to do to keep from moving here?*

Countless possibilities flitted in and out of her mind, but she dismissed them as impractical. Not one solid idea presented itself before her father returned.

"I've traded it," he announced, pointing, "for that 1929 Star coupe over there."

"A coupe? We can't get all us kids in that!"

"I'm going to cut the back out and put a box on it, like a pickup. Now, help me get my tools out of this one, and we'll be on our way home."

They had barely driven a mile when Hildy's father began muttering, "This is a pitiful excuse for a car. It hasn't got the running gears of a katydid! I probably shouldn't have traded the Rickenbacker, especially since that garage man didn't want to give me anything to boot.

"He started out asking $60 for this thing. I told him it was worth $25 tops, and the Rickenbacker was worth a whole lot more. But if he'd give me fifteen dollars cash to boot, I'd trade cars."

Hildy remembered the dollar she'd loaned her father. "Fifteen dollars is a lot of money," she said, trying to avoid asking for the loan to be repaid.

"I didn't get fifteen, only ten. That'll buy some groceries, but I can't repay the dollar I owe you until I get my first paycheck. That okay?"

Hildy was disappointed, but she nodded. "Sure."

*Everything's going from bad to worse!* Hildy thought.

Suddenly, she brightened as a thought gave her hope. *I'll talk*

*to the preacher tomorrow. Maybe he knows where Daddy can get a job
so we won't have to move.*

Hildy began to think excitedly about that possibility as the
Star putted on toward Lone River. But she hadn't counted on
the surprise that waited at the Corrigans' home.

# Chapter Eleven

# A Clash of Wills

When the Star turned into the driveway at the Corrigans' rented house near Lone River, Hildy exclaimed, "That's Mr. Farnham's car! I wonder what he's doing here?"

"I don't know. Let's go inside and find out."

As father and daughter stepped through the front door, Hildy saw that Spud was with the banker.

"What's the matter?" she ask anxiously. "Has something happened to Brother Ben?"

Mr. Farnham absently fingered the heavy gold watch chain stretched across his gray vest. "He's fine," the banker quickly assured her. "But he phoned me awhile ago to ask if Spud and I would bring a message to you."

Spud explained, "Ben had to postpone his trip to the mountains until next week. The doctor doesn't want him to drive the horse trailer up, so Ben's looking for a driver. As soon as he finds one, Ben's taking Buster up to his friends. He still wants you to ride up with him."

Hildy glanced at her father. He slowly shook his head. "I don't think you should go, Hildy. The weather's too uncertain."

84

"But, Mr. Corrigan," Spud said, "I know Ben wouldn't go if the weather were bad. Besides, it's Christmas vacation, so Hildy wouldn't miss school. And it's only a one-day trip. We'll have her home by nightfall."

Hildy's interest perked up. "We?" she repeated.

Spud nodded. "I'm going along. So's Ruby. Uncle Matt and I already talked to her father, and he's given permission."

Hildy turned imploring eyes on her father, but he again shook his head. "The radio's forecasting more storms. In the mountains that means snow. If I let you go and you got caught, the roads could be closed. Maybe you couldn't get back for days. Besides, Molly and I need you to help pack so we can move next week."

Hildy desperately tried again. "You said yourself those weather forecasters are not right very often. Besides, this'll be the last time I can be with my friends, because we won't be here for Christmas. Couldn't I go?"

Joe Corrigan sighed and looked at his wife. Hildy saw Molly nod ever so slightly.

"Oh, I guess so," he answered.

---

The next morning, a brisk wind had blown the fog away. Bright sunshine scoured the blue bowl of sky until it sparkled. By the time a neighbor picked up Hildy and her sisters for the ride to church, Hildy had focused on one last possible chance: talking to the pastor in hopes he would know of a job in Lone River.

As she got out of the car, Hildy saw the preacher just leaving the parsonage next door. She rushed across the small, winter-brown lawn to meet him.

"Pastor Hyde," she began, "I've just got to talk to you about something. Could you please give me five minutes after church?"

"I'd be happy to talk, Hildy, but Sunday's always very busy. How about tomorrow?"

"I may not be able to get a ride into town, and it's real, real important."

He hesitated, apparently reading the anxiety in her young face. "If you can wait until after I've shaken hands with everyone at the door, my wife and I could meet with you in the little room to the right of the pulpit."

Hildy thanked him as older parishioners stepped forward to greet him. Feeling hopeful, Hildy hurried back toward the church. She stopped, surprised to see Glenn Masters get out of a Dodge sedan at the curb.

"Hi!" Glenn greeted her. "You go to church here?"

"I'm a member. Are you going to be a visitor today?"

He nodded. "My folks and I are." He introduced a tall, big-boned man in an old brown suit that smelled of mothballs. Mrs. Masters was a short, stout woman who had bright blue eyes and a warm smile.

After they had exchanged pleasantries, Mr. and Mrs. Masters excused themselves and started up the steep stairs into the church. Hildy and Glenn followed.

Glenn asked casually, "Where's your cousin?"

"Ruby's father preaches at another church in town, so she attends there."

"Oh, I see." The boy's voice showed his disappointment.

Hildy said, "You'll be in my Sunday school class. You already know some of the members from school." She pointed. "See them over there?"

As they walked toward them, Hildy heard the familiar sound of a Model T Ford slowing. She turned as the topless old prewar vehicle shuddered to a stop at the curb. Hildy smiled and waved at her Uncle Nate behind the wheel. He waved back as his daughter stepped to the curb, then drove away.

"Hi!" Hildy greeted her cousin. "I thought you had to attend church with your father."

"I was a-plannin' to go thar—uh—there, but last night after Mr. Farnham and Spud dropped you off, they come—uh—came by our house an' told muh daddy what Ben said to ye about goin'—going—to the mountains. I figured you'd want to make plans, so Daddy let me come here so you'n—we—could talk."

Hildy was pleased, then realized Ruby had been talking to her but looking at Glenn.

He sauntered over, smiling at Ruby. "Hi! Hildy told me you didn't go to this church," he began.

"I come—uh—came to talk to Hildy. We're goin'—going—to the mountains in a day or so."

Hildy dropped back a step, but Ruby and Glenn didn't seem to notice. They walked on together. Hildy frowned. *I wonder if she knew Glenn was going to attend church here today? Or did she really come to talk to me? It doesn't matter. What matters is whether Pastor Hyde can help Daddy get a job so we won't have to move away. And, of course, that Brother Ben's health improves.*

During Sunday school in the musty-smelling basement, Ruby and Glenn sat together. Hildy saw them exchanging sly glances and little smiles. Most of all, Hildy noticed that when Ruby whispered to Glenn, she was very careful to speak better English.

Hildy almost wanted to smile, but she had too much on her mind to dwell on how Ruby and Glenn were getting on.

During the break between Sunday school and church, Hildy looked around for the old ranger. He was nowhere in sight. *I hope he's not worse*, Hildy thought, and quickly said a silent prayer for him.

During the church service, Ruby and Glenn sat together again, and Hildy sat with them, thinking of what she'd say to the pastor. She was barely aware of the small choir's hymns and she only vaguely heard the scripture reading. During Pastor Hyde's sermon on the events leading up to the Christ child's birth, Hildy suddenly stiffened with an idea.

*Of course!* The thought shot through her head with an electric excitement. *Why didn't I think of that before?*

She leaned over to whisper to Ruby, but Glenn's and her eyes had locked, and they both smiled shyly.

Hildy sighed. She felt good that her tomboy cousin had suddenly started showing an interest in boys besides taunting them with the challenge that she could do anything they could. At the same time, Hildy felt a little tinge of concern, because she desperately wanted to share her new idea with Ruby.

When the service ended, Hildy whispered, "Ruby, I've got to talk to you right away."

"Couldn't it wait a bit?" Ruby asked, her eyes on Glenn. Three older members had converged on him, shaking his hand and bidding him welcome.

Hildy wanted to say *No, it can't*. Instead, she said, "I guess so. I'll be in the little room to the right of the altar waiting for Pastor and Sister Hyde. Try to get there before they do."

Hildy walked down the right aisle, past the end of the curved walnut-stained altar, and entered the small room. Sometimes it was filled with people who'd answered the pastor's altar call, but there had been none today. The room was empty, except for several chairs, some books in a case, and one large poster on the wall. It depicted a globe being supported by many hands with the slogan: "It isn't heavy if we all lift."

Hildy sat in one of the chairs and stared thoughtfully at the picture. Right now, she wasn't interested in helping lift the world. She just wanted to have some help in solving her own problems.

Through the closed door, sounds of conversation grew fainter as people filed out of the church. Hildy was still staring moodily at the poster when the door opened slightly. Hildy turned and motioned her cousin to come in.

Ruby said, "I jist met Glenn's folks. They're nice."

Hildy nodded. "I met them, too." She rapidly changed the subject. "I thought of something that might help Brother Ben catch that man who ambushed him."

"Ye did?" Ruby's interest suddenly shifted to focus fully on her cousin. "What?"

"Remember that house on Maple Street near the school where that man chased me and I lost my coat?"

When Ruby nodded, Hildy continued in a rush. "Well, I

don't know why I didn't think of it before, but if we could find out who lives there, maybe he could tell us something about Zane Vernon."

Ruby's hazel eyes lit up. "Yeah, that makes sense! Only, how ye going to do that? You cain't jist walk up to the door and ask."

"I haven't figured that out yet. But there's got to be a way—" she broke off as the door opened and the pastor and his wife entered.

Ruby stood up. "I'll wait for ye outside."

Hildy nodded, stood, and thanked the pastor and his wife for seeing her. As the door closed behind Ruby, the couple took chairs facing Hildy and asked how they could help. She briefly told about her problem.

"So," she finished with a deep breath, "I hope you can help my father find a job so we don't have to move away from Lone River."

The minister cleared his throat. "Have you asked God what His will is in this matter, Hildy?"

The question rankled, just as it had the first time Brother Ben had asked it. "No," she replied.

The pastor's wife said in her soft, quiet voice, "One of the hardest things we have to do in life is remember what the Bible says about God's ways not being our ways, for His thoughts are higher than ours."

Her husband nodded. "For example, Joseph didn't want to be sold into slavery down in Egypt. Yet the Bible tells us that God had a plan for Joseph being there.

"I'm sure Daniel didn't like it a bit when he and his friends were carried away captive. Then Daniel was thrown into a lion's den. But God was with him, and everything turned out fine.

What about Paul the Apostle? A lot of terrible things happened to him, including being shipwrecked, beaten, left for dead, and imprisoned. Yet in that dungeon he wrote letters that still influence millions of people nearly two thousand years later, because God was with him.

"As Paul said, 'I have learned, in whatever state I am, therewith to be content.' Paul learned acceptance. Do you understand what we're saying, Hildy?"

She nodded, feeling keen disappointment. "You're saying I should obey my parents and quit fighting to stay in Lone River."

Sister Hyde explained gently, "We're trying to help you deal with a difficult situation, and asking you to seek God's will instead of your own. Will you do that?"

Hildy's insides churned so that she wanted to cry, *No! I don't want to leave all my friends and move away, so how can it be God's will?* Instead, she slowly stood. "I'll think about it," she promised.

Frustration boiled inside Hildy as she walked through the darkened church to the front door. Ruby and her father waited there. After exchanging greetings with the pastor and his wife, Hildy's Uncle Nate announced that he would drive Hildy home so the girls could finish their conversation.

As Uncle Nate turned on the ignition prior to cranking the Ford, Ruby said she had good news.

"I could use some good news," Hildy admitted as she slid into the open front seat beside her cousin.

"Well," Ruby explained, "while ye were talkin' to the preacher an' his missus, I tol' muh daddy what you said to me in the little room. I mean, about wonderin' who lives in that house where you got chased, an' lost yore coat. He come up with a right good idee."

Hildy listened as Ruby briefly explained, then waited in thoughtful silence while her uncle gave the crank a couple of turns. When the motor started, making the whole car shudder, he hurried around the driver's side and climbed behind the steering wheel.

"Uncle Nate," she said uneasily, "I appreciate your thinking of a way, but it could be dangerous."

He nodded, carefully checked to make sure there was no traffic, then made a U-turn at the intersection. "Maybe, but the good Lord could make it easy too."

He accelerated down the street, adding, "Anyway, hang on to your hats, because we're about to find out!"

## CHAPTER
## TWELVE

---

# HIGH COUNTRY CLUE

Hildy shivered as the Model T continued down the main street. However, she wasn't sure if she shivered from the cold, or fear of what her uncle was about to do.

Ruby said, "The minute I saw ye comin' outta the church with the preacher and his wife I knew they couldn't he'p ye."

Hildy repeated what she had been told. "That was my last hope for helping Daddy find a job here."

"I cain't stand the thought of you movin' away. It makes me sad clean down to my socks."

"Me, too," Hildy admitted as her uncle turned onto Maple Street. "Especially just before Christmas."

Ruby brightened. "Maybe Ben'll leave you somethin' in his will."

Hildy answered somewhat sharply, "I told you not to talk like that!" She softened her tone and added, "What he has belongs to his children and grandchildren. Besides, I don't want anything from him except what he's already given me: love, friendship, and prayers. The one thing I do want is what neither he nor anybody else can give me: a way for my family to stay in Lone River."

The girls fell silent as Nate Konning eased the car to the curb in front of the house where Zane Vernon had chased Hildy and she'd lost her coat. She watched apprehensively as her uncle climbed the steps.

Hildy scooted lower in the seat when the door opened to his knock. A man almost as tall and thin as Uncle Nate peered through the screen.

Hildy could barely hear her uncle's words: "I'm Nate Konning, pastor of the Lone River Bible Church, and I'm looking for Zane Vernon. Can you help me?"

The man said, "Funny you should ask. An old gentleman was here awhile ago asking the same thing."

"Brother Ben," Hildy said, and Ruby nodded.

"I told him no," the thin man in the house continued. "But after he was gone, I thought of something."

"What's that?" Nate asked.

"A fellow by the name of Vernon showed up here a few days back, wanting to sell me some beef for my store."

"Store?" Nate asked.

"I own one in Dos Piedras, but I'm semi-retired, so my son runs it. This Vernon fellow wanted to sell some beef carcasses, but Dan—that's my son—sent him to me. I told him that we have our own regular suppliers."

"Did he give you any way to get in touch with him?"

Hildy tensed, straining to hear the answer.

"Yes, but I didn't figure on ever contacting him, so I didn't pay much attention. After the old gentleman that asked about him was gone, I remembered something that Vernon left here. Step inside and I'll show you."

The man opened the door and Nate went inside.

Ruby asked, "What do ye reckon that means?"

"I guess we'll find out soon," Hildy answered, trying to keep her teeth from chattering in the topless car. She anxiously watched the house until her uncle reappeared. "My coat!" she cried. "He's got my coat!"

"Guess what?" Nate said, handing it to Hildy. "This was hanging on the rack inside the front door. The man said he found it on the street. He figured some kid lost it, so he was going to take it to the school but never got around to it. When I told him it was yours, he gave it to me."

Hildy gratefully slipped into it. "Did he tell you how to get in touch with Zane Vernon?" she asked.

Her uncle handed Hildy a piece of paper. "Sure did, and in Vernon's own handwriting."

Hildy glanced at the crude letters and read aloud: "Messages: Jake Jessup, phone J–1–0–3, Timber Meadows." Hildy looked up at her uncle. "Timber Meadows is where Brother Ben's friend lives. And that name—Jessup—I think that's the name of the man who claimed Vernon had stolen his truck. Maybe Brother Ben was right, and there is a connection."

Nate said, "Let's drive by Ben's place before I take you home."

When the old ranger opened the door, Hildy was excited and hopeful. Ben invited the visitors in and listened to their explanation for being there. Then he took the piece of paper from Hildy and studied it.

"Hmmm." He nodded, tapping the paper with his right forefinger. "Because we haven't seen Vernon around here lately, and there've been no reports of cattle rustling, I wonder if Vernon might be with Jessup."

"Could you check it out when we take Buster up to the high country?" Hildy asked.

Ben replied, "It'd be a hard push to do all that in one day. But my friend Quint has a phone, so I could at least check with the sheriff's office while we're there.

"Which reminds me," he continued, "I talked to a truck driver named Stubby. He'll drive Buster up to Quint's, but he can't do that until Thursday. Can you girls ride up with Spud and me on that day?"

Hildy's heart sagged. "We may be moved by then, or at least

we'll be packing. Daddy says he wants to be in the new place before Christmas, which is next Tuesday."

"I'm surprised he wouldn't want to stay here through the holidays," Ben said.

Ruby declared, "Ye don't know Uncle Joe. When he takes a notion to do somethin', he up and does it."

"Maybe something will happen to give you time to make the trip to Timber Meadows with us," Ben said.

Hildy nodded, but didn't hold much hope. When her uncle and cousin dropped her off at home, Hildy saw her father's feet sticking out from under the Star.

She could hear his angry muttering as he slid out into full view. With only a nod of acknowledgement to the two visitors, he grumbled, "This car is the nearest thing to nothing I ever saw in my life! I should never have traded for it."

"What's the matter, Daddy?" Hildy asked.

"Everything! Blasted pile of junk won't run, and I can't find out why!" He turned a disgusted look at the Star, then looked back to his visitors. "Well, there's nothing more I can do right now. Why don't you all come in. Molly's kept your meal hot, Hildy."

As the cousins followed their fathers toward the house, Ruby whispered, "Ye reckon he cain't get it fixed until after Thursday?"

"I hope not," Hildy said, then immediately felt guilty. But she wanted desperately to make the trip to the high country, so she didn't dwell on her guilt.

The next day the fog was back. Hildy's father determined that the Star needed major repairs, including parts. But he had no money, so he walked into town. That night he told his wife and oldest daughters that he had traded two days' work as a mechanic at the local repair shop for the necessary parts.

Hildy thought quickly. "That'll take until Wednesday night. Then how long to install the parts on the Star?"

"One day, maybe less. So you may as well go with Ben and your friends on Thursday. But in the meantime, you can help pack so we can move by Friday for sure."

The fog continued through Wednesday afternoon when a stiff breeze blew it away. Thursday morning, Molly awakened Hildy at dawn. "Better get dressed. Ben'll be here soon. It's clear outside, so it looks as if you'll have a beautiful day for your trip to the mountains. But another storm's coming Friday. Anyway, that's what your father heard yesterday on the radio at the garage."

Hildy smiled. "You know what Daddy says: You can't depend on those radio forecasters. They're wrong more than they're right."

After dressing, Hildy went to the barn and climbed up to the rafters to check on the red box. *I don't know what I'm going to put in this*, she thought. *Daddy can't repay the dollar he owes me, so I can't buy Molly anything. But maybe I'll think of something else I can give her between now and when we open our presents.*

Hildy was ready when Ben arrived in the Packard. "See you tonight," Hildy called to her family, as she slid into the front seat with Ruby and the old ranger. She smiled at Spud sitting in the backseat.

"Where's the driver with Buster?" Hildy asked as the car crunched onto the county road.

Ben replied, "Stubby's truck is a lot slower than this car, so I sent him on ahead. We'll catch up and probably pass him before we get through the foothills."

Ruby prompted, "Ben, ye was telling us the other day about capturing Vernon a long time ago, but ye didn't tell how he excaped and bushwhacked you."

The old ranger gripped the steering wheel so hard his knuckles turned white. "I don't feel like talking about it just now. Maybe later."

He added, "I didn't sleep too well last night because I was thinking about Zane Vernon's friend, Jake Jessup. It's almost too much to hope for, but I certainly would like to find Vernon while we're on this trip."

Hildy anxiously glanced at the old ranger. "You're not thinking of trying to catch him today, are you?"

"Nothing would give me greater satisfaction than to see him back behind bars! But if I locate him, I'll notify the sheriff's office and let them handle it."

When he stopped in a small foothill community for gasoline, Ben stayed at the pump to watch the attendant fill the gas tank. Hildy buttoned her coat and stepped out of the car in front of the combination service station and cafe. Ruby and Spud followed.

As they stepped gingerly across the oil-splattered dirt driveway, Ruby glanced over her shoulder at the old ranger, then lowered her voice. "It's all well an' good to want to clear his name, but what if Ben finds Vernon up in the mountains and cain't call the sheriff? What's an 85-year-old man gonna do ag'in someone like that?"

Spud opened the door to the cafe. "He's a very resourceful old gentleman; he'd find a way."

"But suppose somethin' goes wrong?" Ruby persisted. "What if'n Zane does what he done before an' shoots Ben? We could git hurt, too."

"Let's talk about something else," Hildy suggested, fighting off a shiver.

"Yeah," Ruby agreed. "Like I'm shore—sure—glad your folks didn't move away so ye—you—could ride up with us today."

Spud commented, "It's gratifying to hear you correcting your English, Ruby."

Hildy expected Ruby to flare up and declare it was none of Spud's business. Instead, Ruby just smiled. Hildy noticed a sudden faint tinge of color in Ruby's cheeks. Hildy knew that Glenn Masters was having more of an impact on Ruby than the teachers' or the principal's threats.

When they were all back in the Packard and again headed toward the high country, the topic returned to Hildy's family moving away.

Hildy said, "When we came to Lone River, we just wanted

a little land where we could plant a garden, raise some chickens, have a cow for milk, and not have to move for years—maybe even find our 'forever' home."

She paused, sighed, then shrugged. "I've done all I can to keep from moving away. There's nothing else I can think of to do, and I'm sick inside about it."

Ben pointed through the windshield. "There's Stubby in his truck with Buster."

The Packard pulled alongside the driver. Ben exchanged a friendly wave with Stubby. He had a fierce black moustache and a battered, gray cowboy hat. Ben speeded up, and soon the truck with the horse was lost to sight on the narrow, curving mountain road.

Some time later they came to Timber Meadows. The old ranger turned off the highway into a long, narrow dirt driveway and parked in front of a weathered house that stood in the middle of a flat, winter-brown meadow. The house's steeply pitched roof was made of rusted corrugated metal. Snow could slide off easily, but there was no snow except on the mountain peaks.

A large corral of stout cedar posts and lodgepole pine trunks surrounded two low barns. Hildy's nose told her that many horses had been quartered there, but none were visible.

Hildy stepped out of the car, instantly aware of the cold at the high altitude. She hastily buttoned her coat while smelling woodsmoke mixed with the fresh, clean fragrance of towering pines. Her eyes swept on, past stately old cedars and fir trees scattered over the half-mile-wide meadow. Its edge was marked in all directions by blue-gray mountains that rose up sharply, showing conifers on the sides to timberline. From there to the snowcovered peaks, there were only immense, barren, granite boulders.

"It's beautiful," Hildy said softly, "except for that sky. It's clouding up fast."

The front door opened and a powerfully built man of medium height stepped out of the house and hurried toward the new arrivals. He was dressed in a heavy sheepskin coat, gray cowboy hat, and scuffed boots. He had a broad chest but almost no hips. His old blue jeans seemed about ready to fall off.

"Ben, you old horsefly!" he cried jovially, wrapping the old ranger in a bear hug and pounding him on the back. "I'm mighty glad to see you."

"Same here, Quint," Ben replied, solidly thumping his old friend in return.

When the two men had separated, Ben said, "Quint, this is Hildy, Ruby, and Spud. They're great kids to have along."

"Howdy," Quint boomed, giving Spud a hearty handshake and tipping his hat to the girls. "Come in! Come in! My missus will warm your insides while Ben and me catch up on all the news since we last talked."

As he started toward the house, Quint turned back to face the old ranger. "Oh, Ben, the man who's driving your horse up in the truck called awhile ago from a pay phone. He broke down, but says he's sure he can make repairs and be here by nightfall."

"Nightfall?" Hildy echoed. "We're supposed to be home before then!"

Quint shook his head. "Sorry, Hildy, but you may all be here longer than overnight."

"How come?" she asked in sudden concern.

"Because we just got the news on the radio that a fast-moving snowstorm's coming in," Quint replied. "It's supposed to be a big one. Looks like you folks could be snowbound here for the next couple of days."

# CHAPTER
## THIRTEEN
---

# MOUNTAIN PERILS

"Snowbound, Mr. Armstrong?" Hildy echoed the word as she followed him past firewood stacked five feet high under the covered porch.

"Yes," Quint replied, opening the front door and motioning the guests inside. He added, "At least, that's what the radio weatherman said this morning. Either way, don't worry. Our kids are grown and gone, so we have beds for all of you."

"That's very kind," Hildy said, "but our families will worry if we don't get home tonight."

"We'll call your folks and tell them you'll all be home when the roads are cleared again."

A graying woman, round as a butter churn, waddled out of the kitchen, trailed by the fragrance of baking cookies. "Ben!" she exclaimed, wiping her hands on her apron, then shaking his hand. "It's wonderful to see you! And thanks for bringing these young people. It never seems like Christmas without a houseful of them."

"Martha," the old ranger replied with a warm smile, "it's always good to see one of my favorite women."

She made a flustered motion with her hands. "Go along with you, now! You'll turn my head so's I won't be able to do a lick of work the rest of this blessed day."

"How's the family?" he asked.

Mrs. Armstrong answered, "All seven of our children and twelve grandchildren are well, thank you. But I declare, sometimes I wish the good Lord had let them live close, instead of scattered across the country. Not one of them is going to make it home this Christmas."

Hildy instantly liked Mr. and Mrs. Armstrong. He took their coats and hung them beside the door. She invited them to follow her.

At a glance Hildy could see that this was not a fancy house, but it was definitely a home. It had that special feeling that stirred longings deep within her heart.

As they crossed the living room, Hildy saw it was heated by a large potbellied stove in the far corner. A battery-operated radio rested on a small table beside the large davenport, which faced a matching chair and padded rocker.

Behind the chairs, floor-to-ceiling shelves were filled with books. Two kerosene lamps with polished reflectors were mounted on the wall. They were surrounded with family photographs. There were more on the fireplace mantle, along with knickknacks, a clock, and other homey touches. Everything matched Mrs. Armstrong's pleasant, motherly personality.

Hildy's whole being responded to this sense of place, a particular house and land that was more than where someone lived. It made Hildy ache for her own "forever" home.

In a home like that, emotional roots would run deep. They'd run so deep that even if some family members could not get home for the holidays they knew it was there. It waited for them, solid and loving, a secure and permanent spot in the world that was forever special because it was really a home. It would always call them back with invisible bonds so strong only death would sever them.

That made her think of Brother Ben's illness and that tomor-

row her family planned to move away from Lone River and all
that Hildy held dear.

She felt her eyes grow hot with bittersweet tears, realizing
that she was now in someone's "forever" home, but her own
was denied her. Tomorrow she and her family would again be
rootless in this sacred season, her dream of a "forever" home
more remote than ever.

Hildy's eyes lingered longingly on the white fir Christmas
tree in the corner opposite the stove. The tree was decorated
with popcorn and fresh cranberries that had been strung on
thread. A few colorfully wrapped gifts were arranged beneath
the tree. Hildy's family not only didn't have a tree, but there
wouldn't be many presents either, and Hildy knew the opportunity to get something for Molly was almost gone.

She tried not to think about such sad things as she followed
Mrs. Armstrong into her spacious kitchen. It held a huge range
with a polished cooking top, a hot water reservoir, and full-
width warming closet. A few steps away from the long drain
boards on either side of the sink with its short-handled pump,
a table was set with white napkins and blue-willow English
China.

"Sit! Sit!" Mrs. Armstrong urged, motioning to the six Wind-
sor chairs placed around the table. "I have hot cocoa for you
young people. There's coffee for us older folks, and freshly
baked oatmeal cookies for everybody."

"May Ruby and I help?" Hildy asked.

"Oh, land sakes, no! I can manage. You girls sit down with
the men. It'll only take me a minute to get things on the table."

When all the guests were seated, Quint stepped to the far
end of the table and dropped heavily into a chair. His back was
to the window at the front of the house.

"Martha," he said to his wife, "if you'll join us for a moment,
I'll give thanks."

He reached out with a calloused hand and took Spud's with
his left and Hildy's with his right. The circle was completed
when Mrs. Armstrong held Ruby's and Ben's hands.

When Quint's brief prayer ended, he looked at Ben. "Tell me

about these young friends of yours, and then fill me in on what's going on in your—"

"Car's coming," his wife interrupted, looking beyond the table to the window. She got up and quickly lifted the corner of the curtain to peer out. "Why, it's a couple of deputy sheriffs. I wonder what they want?"

"I'll go find out," her husband said. He excused himself and left the room. "The rest of you go ahead."

They obliged as Mrs. Armstrong silently passed a plate of cookies. Nobody at the table spoke, but listened instead. Hildy could make out only a low murmur of voices.

When Quint reappeared, every eye focused on him. "Nothing to get excited about, folks," he announced, sitting down again. "The deputies said they'd been chasing three cattle rustlers at the far end of our meadow. Caught two, but one got—"

"Cattle rustlers?" Ben interrupted.

"Uh-huh. One got away. The deputies say he'll have to seek shelter from the storm. They think he'll probably slip back into town. But the officers wanted to warn me in case he comes here instead."

Hildy noticed the old ranger's blue eyes were bright with excitement. He asked, "Did the deputies mention any of those rustlers' names?"

Quint shook his head. "No." He glanced sharply at the old ranger. "Why? You know something about this?"

Ben briefly explained while everyone else ate cookies and sipped on their hot beverages.

When he had finished, Quint suggested, "Why don't you call the sheriff's office and ask if they know who they are? Phone's on the kitchen wall."

The old ranger stood and went to the black phone. He rang for the operator and asked for the sheriff's office. Hildy and the others listened while Ben explained who he was and what he wanted to know. When he returned to the table, Hildy noticed the excitement in his eyes.

He said quietly, "They caught one man named Jake Jessup

and another called Al. The one who got away was Zane Vernon."

Hildy felt the silent alarm bells going off in her head. She looked anxiously at Ruby and Spud and read the same concern in their faces.

Ben added in his soft drawl, "Quint, I'd be obliged if you'd show me around your place, just in case Vernon does show up here."

There was such a quiet, ominous tone to his voice that Hildy's heart began speeding up. "I'd like to go with you," she said.

Shortly thereafter, bundled up against the frigid air, Hildy, Ruby, and Spud followed Ben and Quint outside. The sky was totally overcast.

Quint commented, "This place keeps Martha and me pretty busy now that the kids are grown and gone, but we wouldn't live anywhere else."

Hildy nodded, thinking, *That's how I feel about Lone River.* She shook off the thought and listened to Quint as he pointed out various features of the ranch.

The meadow was covered with white fir, cedar, Jeffrey and sugar pine. Quint had cut a young white fir for the Christmas tree. Older white firs that had fallen had been cut for firewood, now stacked on the porch.

Quint said that the two-foot wide, blackened corral posts were from cedar trees that had burned in a forest fire. That preserved them so that insects and rot didn't affect the posts. The corral rails between the posts were made of twelve-foot sections of tamarack trees. They were about equal in diameter on both ends, making a stout but uniform fence.

Spud said, "I read that those really are lodgepole pines, and California doesn't have any true tamaracks."

"That's right," Quint admitted. "They're lodgepole, but around here we call them tamaracks. Man named Salter helped put them in years ago. When he moved on, he did much the same thing at his place."

The old ranger asked casually, "Where's he live?"

Quint pointed to the nearest mountain range. "Up in the primitive area near Devil's Backbone. He's a hermit. Some people say he's ornery and cantankerous and not quite right in the head. But a man who loves horses as he does can't be all bad."

Ben asked, "Is this the only house around here?"

"Yes, unless you count Salty's place," Quint said. He pointed out the harness shed, tack room, tall hay barn, and two low horse barns.

Hildy asked, "Mr. Armstrong, where are your horses?"

"I sent them over to Nevada a couple of days ago. Ben, it's too bad your horse couldn't have been here by then. But I'll see that he gets over in a few days."

"How come you take them to Nevada?" Ruby asked,

"It's high desert, with less snow. Here the drifts get so high that sometimes a horse steps in a hole and breaks a leg. But don't worry, Ben. I'll keep your horse in the barn or corral until the weather breaks. Then he can go to Nevada until spring."

Hildy was puzzled. "We had horses back east, and they stayed through the winter snows. So how come it's different here?"

"These Sierras are more than a mile high, and sometimes the drifts get so deep they'll even block a train," Quint explained. He changed the subject, pointing out cedars and sugar pines he estimated to be between 150 and 180 feet tall.

The tour ended back at the front porch just as a truck pulled off the highway, heading toward the house.

"Here comes my horse," Ben announced, waving to the approaching driver. "I'm sure glad he beat the storm."

Hildy joined the others in surrounding the truck as the short, balding driver climbed down from the high cab. Ben introduced him as "Stubby Malone, the best truck driver I ever met."

"Thanks for the kind words," Stubby replied, walking with a bowlegged gait to the back of the truck. "But I want to get unloaded so I can make tracks out of here."

Quint shook his head. "I hope you're not going to try beating this storm back to the valley."

"I know better than that. I've got friends in Reno. I figure I can make it across there ahead of the snow."

Buster had made the trip in good shape, Hildy decided when the old ranger backed the gelding down the ramp and onto the ground.

Hildy walked over and affectionately patted the horse's neck. "I'm glad you're here, Buster," she said softly. She turned to Ben and raised her voice: "I'll put him in the barn," she offered. "The rest of you go on inside where it's warm."

"Much obliged, Hildy, but I'd like to do it myself," Ben said.

She nodded in understanding. Ben gripped Buster's halter and led him toward the barn. Hildy walked silently beside him as the others entered the house.

The wind whistled shrilly through cracks in the horse barn, but the shelter was noticeably warmer than outside. "Brother Ben," she began, removing a horse blanket from a metal railing, "I've been watching you carefully. What are you thinking?"

He helped her secure the blanket over Buster before answering. "Zane Vernon's got to find shelter, and there are only two places he can do that around here."

Hildy used a pitchfork to place sweet-smelling hay in the manger. "You mean here and the hermit's place?"

"That's too far away, but Vernon surely will see the smoke from Quint's house and head this way. And when he does, I'll be waiting for him."

Hildy looked sharply at the old ranger. He seemed calm, but Hildy's heart began thudding like a drum.

Later, Spud phoned Matt Farnham to explain why they couldn't get home that night. The banker said he'd drive over and tell Hildy's and Ruby's fathers, since they had no phone.

The adults decided to make the house look normal in case Vernon showed up. That included sending Hildy, Ruby, and Spud to bed. Eventually, the adults would blow out the lamp so it would appear as if everyone were asleep.

Mrs. Armstrong showed the reluctant Spud down a long hallway to a bedroom that her sons had once occupied. The girls were given another bedroom, where the Armstrongs' daughters had slept.

Hildy and Ruby quickly removed one layer of clothing in the unheated room and slid under the heavy covers. Soon Ruby was asleep, but Hildy was wakeful. She undid her braids and lay there until she heard the storm break. The wind drowned out any possibility of her hearing Vernon if he tried to break in through the window. Hildy folded her hands under the covers and closed her eyes.

*Lord,* she prayed silently, *I know that Brother Ben wants to capture Zane Vernon and remove the stain on his record. Brother Ben says he doesn't have too long to live, but please protect him and the rest of us.*

Hildy thought about her family moving away, and those who had urged her to say, "Not my will, but Thine be done." But Hildy couldn't bring herself to say that.

She hadn't expected to sleep at all, so she was surprised to be awakened by Mrs. Armstrong, who held a lamp in one hand. "Hildy, Ruby! Wake up!"

Alarmed, Hildy sat bolt upright, but Ruby only muttered in her sleep.

"What's wrong?" Hildy asked anxiously.

"That outlaw—"

"Zane Vernon!" Hildy interrupted, suddenly wide awake. "Did they catch him?"

"No, but he was here and stole Ben's horse."

Hildy jumped out of bed. "He did?"

Mrs. Armstrong nodded. "Ben's going after him at first light."

"Oh, no!" Hildy breathed, reaching for her clothes.

"Quint fell and twisted his knee, so he can't help. We don't want Ben to go alone, but he won't listen. Can you talk him out of it?"

"I'll try," Hildy said grimly. She added silently, *But if I fail, I hate to think what could happen.*

# Chapter Fourteen

# ON THE OUTLAW'S TRAIL

Hildy hastily dressed and coaxed her sleepy and reluctant cousin to do the same. Hildy didn't stop to braid her long brown hair. It spilled over her shoulders. "I'm going to cut my hair short the first chance I get," she grumbled, peering out the bedroom window. It had stopped snowing. She shook the hair out of her eyes and entered the Armstrongs' kitchen with Ruby. A kerosene lamp burned in the middle of the table because it was not quite daylight. In a quick glance, Hildy saw Spud looking out the window, the old ranger at the wall telephone, and Mr. and Mrs. Armstrong sitting at the table. Quint Armstrong grimaced with pain.

"What happened?" Hildy asked anxiously.

Quint explained, "We heard Ben's horse whinny, so we ran outside with the flashlight. The barn door was open. Buster was gone, but his tracks were fresh. We started following them, when I tripped and twisted my knee. Ben had to help me get back inside." Quint pointed to a damp bath towel resting on his knee. "Martha's packed it in snow to keep the swelling down."

The old ranger seemed all right as he replaced the receiver on its hook. He was fully dressed, except for his hat and coat. "I can't raise the operator," he said, "so we can't call the sheriff. Quint can't go anywhere with that bum leg, and Martha can't drive for help."

Martha said, "I'll keep trying the phone, but I wish you'd sit down and wait for the deputies."

"Yes!" Hildy exclaimed. "Please wait."

"Sorry, I can't do that," Ben said. "I'm obliged for your concern, but I don't think there's too much risk. From what Quint told me, Vernon's got to be heading for that hermit's place. There Vernon will hole up until the weather's better, then probably ride on across the mountains into Reno. Buster can probably take a short ride, but a trip to Nevada would surely kill him."

Quint said, "I know how much that horse means to you, but it's better to lose him than your life."

The old ranger's soft drawl took on a firm edge. "Some things are more important than my health. I never really figured I'd get a chance to clear my name, not after all these years. Suddenly, I've got that chance. I've got to go after Vernon."

"You could get hurt or killed!" Hildy protested.

Ben answered somberly, "Vernon killed my father and ambushed me. You all know that if it hadn't been for Buster, I'd be dead. Now he'll be dead if Vernon rides him too hard in these snowy mountains."

Ben hesitated, then continued. "Vernon will figure nobody's going to follow him in the mountains—especially in this uncertain weather. Maybe he won't push too hard, so I might catch up to him before he reaches Salter's. Anyway, he won't know I'm on his trail, so that's to my advantage. I'm going to get Buster back and bring Vernon in too."

Hildy said impulsively, "Then I'm going with you."

"No!" Ben said sharply. "It could be dangerous."

"No more than having you out there alone."

Spud stepped over to stand with Hildy. "She's right. Ben, if you persist in doing this, I'm going too."

"Same here," Ruby added.

The old ranger shook his head emphatically. "I'm grateful to all of you, but your clothes aren't made for snow country. Your shoes will be useless out there."

"So will your cowboy boots!" Hildy replied, pointing to them. "Snow'll come right over the loose tops, and your feet will freeze."

"Maybe Quint will loan me a pair of laced boots."

Hildy turned to Mrs. Armstrong. "Did any of your children leave boots and warm clothing here?"

"Land sakes, yes! The clothes will fit, but I'd guess their old boots are too big for any of you."

Spud spoke up. "When I was hoboing, I learned how to make footwear fit. Mrs. Armstrong, if you'll show me what boots are available, I think we can make them fit by stuffing the toes with old newspapers or by wearing extra socks."

Mrs. Armstrong rummaged through closets and found suitable clothing and boots for everyone. Then she went to make breakfast while the guests dressed.

Hildy didn't like borrowing a comb, but she had no choice. She picked up a comb and brush from the dresser and looked at her hair in the mirror. "I didn't dream we'd be away all night. My hair's really a mess," she said to Ruby. "I'm going to cut it off when I get home!"

*Home!* She sucked in her breath. *I've got no home,* she realized with silent anguish. *At least not in Lone River.* There had been so much excitement this morning that she hadn't remembered that today her family would be moving to Flatsville.

*I won't be there to help them move,* she thought. *Now everybody will be worrying about when we'll get back. Daddy would be real upset if he knew what we're about to do.*

Hildy sighed heavily. *I pray that we all get back safely.*

Back in the kitchen, Quint asked the blessing and special protection for Ben, Hildy, Ruby, Spud, and the hermit, Salter. Then the four guests ate a hearty but hurried breakfast of bacon, eggs, biscuits, and country gravy.

Quint said, "Kids, I've given Ben a map showing a shortcut to Salty's place. While you're on your way there, Martha will keep trying to get through to the sheriff on the telephone. In the meantime, if somebody comes by, we'll send them to get the deputies. They could follow your tracks in the snow. So it'll only be a matter of time until help would be on the way to you—not that I expect you'll need it."

After breakfast Mrs. Armstrong handed each of her guests a paper sack containing a lunch. "I hope you're at Mr. Salter's before noon," she explained, "but if you aren't, it wouldn't be neighborly to barge in unannounced and eat his food."

Quint winced with pain as he twisted in his chair to bid the travelers goodbye. Mrs. Armstrong led the way toward the front door, followed by Ben, Hildy, Ruby, and Spud. They donned mittens and stocking caps as Mrs. Armstrong opened a small closet and retrieved a rifle.

"Ben," she explained, "Quint says bears should be hibernating by now, but you might run across a mountain lion or something." She carefully handed the rifle to the old ranger. "It's not loaded. Here are the shells."

Hildy stared uneasily as the old ranger checked the weapon. "It's an old Springfield Ought-Six," he remarked.

Spud nodded. "I read about that model. It's a 30-caliber, made for the military in 1906 as an improvement over the Ought-Three model. This holds five cartridges, four in the magazine and one in the chamber. There's a quick release trapdoor underneath that drops the extra shells out fast."

"Let's hope we don't need it," Ben said, loading the weapon.

They waved goodbye to Mrs. Armstrong, then skirted the corral fence, heading east toward dense conifers. In less than a hundred yards, Hildy looked back and realized the Armstrongs' house was already out of sight. There was no sound except the crunch of their boots on the snow and a low, moaning sound high in the treetops.

*This is spooky!* Hildy thought, glancing around anxiously. Except for the four of them, there was no sign of any living creature anywhere. There was only a great green-and-white combination of evergreens and snow against a background of soaring mountain peaks that seemed to wait in brooding silence for the travelers.

Ben commented, "Quint says that Vernon must know this country. He wouldn't risk going into it unless he knew he was going to find shelter on the way. Vernon probably plans to hide out at Salter's until it's safe to go on across the summit into Nevada. That would be out of California officers' jurisdiction. If he gets there, they can't touch him. And if Vernon gets to Salter's place before we do, he can hold off an army all by himself. At least that's what Quint told me."

Hildy leaned forward slightly as she followed the old ranger up the first mountain. She asked, "What do you mean, 'If Vernon gets to the hermit's before we do?' "

"Well, if Vernon doesn't push Buster too hard, the shortcut Quint told me about should help us to beat him to Salter's. There I hope to surprise him—so fast that he doesn't even know we're there until he's a prisoner. But that's only if he doesn't push Buster beyond his endurance."

*Or*, Hildy thought grimly, *your health doesn't give out and you collapse in this wilderness*. She shivered, wondering what she, Ruby, and Spud would do if that happened.

Ben added, "Another reason to beat Vernon there is that from what Quint tells me, Salter's ornery streak might make him resist Vernon. Quint says he knows Salter has some guns, but I suspect Vernon has one, too."

Hildy glanced at Ruby and Spud to see if they had received the same ominous, unspoken message she had.

Spud whispered, "He means the recluse could be dead by the time we get there."

Hildy shivered at the thought, but said no more. She saved her breath for climbing the first mountain. Even though she was on a horse trail, it rose steeply at the meadow's edge. Soon her breath rolled out in quick puffs, and her heart pounded with the effort.

The air was sharp and clean, Hildy noticed, as they followed Buster's tracks up ever-steeper slopes. Hildy was concerned about Ben's health, because he was breathing more loudly than anyone else. She was glad when he stopped and pointed to a trampled area in the snow.

"Here's where Vernon let Buster stop and blow. That's good. It shows that Vernon's not pushing him too hard. Buster's too old to carry much weight and move too fast on a snowy mountain trail. It also means Vernon doesn't suspect anyone's behind him."

Suddenly, up ahead, a gunshot sounded.

Ben stiffened as the sound echoed and died away in the distance. "A pistol," he said quietly. "Beyond that next ridge."

"Who do you think fired it?" Hildy asked anxiously.

"Had to be Vernon. We haven't come far enough to be near the hermit's place."

Ruby whispered, "What'd he shoot at?"

Ben's voice took on a hard edge. "Let's hope he didn't shoot Buster. But if Vernon's on foot, maybe we can end this sooner than we expected. No more talking."

The old ranger set such a fast pace that Hildy was sure he'd collapse. Yet he seemed indestructible, even though his breathing was loud and raspy.

The trail narrowed at the top of a ridge, and they formed a single file through immense boulders and scrub brush. Bright sunshine reflected off the snowy peaks. Hildy desperately wanted to rest, but she didn't want to be the one to call for it. She was very glad when the old ranger turned and laid his forefinger across his lips for total silence. Then he motioned for Hildy, Ruby, and Spud to come near. He pointed at some large new tracks alongside Buster's in the snow.

"Mountain lion," Ben whispered, breathing hard. "See how his tracks are on top of the hoofprints? That means the cat came along after Buster passed. The lion is following him."

Hildy stared in fascination at the pug mark. It was round and about as big as a man's fist. She remembered hearing that the big cats love horsemeat, although she doubted that a lion could take a full-grown horse. Still, Hildy cast anxious glances around as Ben shifted the rifle to the ready position, bent low, and eased forward.

Hildy, Ruby, and Spud, also doubled over and followed silently. Hildy's heart had not slowed to normal, and she was still breathing hard when the old ranger stopped again. His breathing was ragged as Hildy and Ruby moved forward to his right. Spud came up on his left. Ben silently pointed past the boy.

"Buster's tracks go down. So do the lion's."

Hildy's eyes followed the two animals' prints down to where the trail narrowed to a few feet wide. The left side ended with a sheer drop-off into a canyon of tumbled boulders, snow, and trees. On the right, just past some lodgepole pines, a lone white fir, and a small stand of burgundy-colored manzanita, a south-facing granite cliff rose straight up about fifty feet.

As Hildy's eyes probed along the trail toward the cliff's end, she heard a strange cry. She knew at once it was from a horse, but it was neither a friendly nicker nor a whinny. It was a scream of pain.

Hildy located the source of the sound at the end of the snowy trail at the base of the cliff just above the canyon's rim. "There!" she whispered, pointing. "There's Buster!"

She looked closer, and her heart seemed to stop.

# Chapter Fifteen

# THE TRAPPED HORSE

Hildy had been around horses much of her life, but she had never seen anything like the scene below. Buster stood on a narrow ledge of the mountain's south-facing slope. His back was to those who watched on the ridge. From shoulders to hips, the gelding was wedged between the face of a granite cliff on his right and an immense boulder on his left.

He struggled mightily to free himself, throwing his head hard to the right. Hildy heard it hit sickeningly against the cliff that rose straight up about 50 feet. Then the buckskin kicked with his left hind hoof, striking the boulder so hard that the iron shoe rang in the still mountain air.

"How'd he get in—?" Hildy whispered, but was interrupted by the horse's scream of pain and fear.

The old ranger's voice cracked like thunder. "That fool Vernon apparently tried to lead him between the boulder and the cliff. Buster got stuck, not able to move forward or backward. So Vernon left him there to die!"

Hildy looked around anxiously. "Where is Vernon?"

"Most likely went ahead on foot to the hermit's place. You

stay here. I'll scout around to make sure."

Spud warned, "Be careful of your footing. That looks like talus between here and there."

"It is," Ben answered, starting down the slope with the rifle. "I'll be careful."

"What's talus?" Ruby asked.

Spud explained, "That's what you call the sloping mass of rocky fragments at the base of that cliff."

Hildy followed the old ranger with anxious eyes as he passed lodgepole pines and manzanita, then the lone white fir. All growth stopped just before the cliff thrust its way up from the trail.

"That trail between the cliff and the edge of that canyon is no more than five feet wide," Hildy guessed.

"Probably slippery with shale under that snow too," Spud added. "That's a mighty dangerous combination."

Hildy was fearful that Ben might slip and fall into the boulder-filled canyon on the left. It dropped down a few hundred yards from the narrow ledge.

Twenty feet from the trapped horse, Ben stopped and looked back. "It's all shale from here on."

Ruby asked, "What's shale?"

Spud told her, "It's thin layers of rock containing clay matter that looks like it's been laminated. Shale pieces slide on each other, much worse than loose rocks."

Hildy watched apprehensively as Ben crossed the shale. He slipped twice, throwing his arms out wide to regain his balance as the footing shifted beneath him. Hildy held her breath until he neared the horse.

Buster tried to turn his head to look back. But he was so pinned in that he could only twist his neck slightly. He made such a strange sound that it seemed to Hildy like a welcome nicker mixed with a shriek of pain.

Hildy said with a crack in her voice, "I've never heard a horse make a sound like that. It tears me up inside."

Buster continued to thrash about, vainly striking out with

his hooves against the cliff and the boulder. Hildy heard Ben speak softly as he gently touched the buckskin's left flank. Then Ben slowly eased between the outside of the boulder and the edge of the cliff. He was within inches of the canyon. He held on to the boulder with his left hand and gripped the rifle in his right. Hildy didn't breathe until he was safely by.

"He made it!" she whispered, adding a swift, silent prayer of gratitude. She watched Ben touch Buster's forehead. Ben drew his left hand back and looked at it. Hildy saw that the hand was bloody.

"Oh, that poor horse!" she murmured. "He must have hurt himself throwing his head around so hard!"

Ben wiped his hand in a snowbank, removed Buster's bridle, then continued cautiously past the gelding and out of sight around the curve. He reappeared a moment later and motioned Hildy, Ruby, and Spud forward.

He stopped them when they got within twenty feet of where he was again examining Buster. "That's close enough. The shale's slick as ice; don't risk falling into the canyon. The trail ends just around that curve. That means Vernon took a wrong turn and had to backtrack, still looking for Salter's place."

Hildy asked, "What are you going to do?"

"Buster's caught in a kind of V-shaped vice, so he can't go forward or backward. I'm going to take off his saddle and blanket."

"I'll help," Spud volunteered.

"Thanks, but I'll manage."

Hildy, Ruby, and Spud watched helplessly as the old ranger crawled across the top of the boulder. He unsuccessfully tried to release the surcingle that secured the saddle, then finally reached down with his pocketknife.

Ruby muttered, "If'n that old hoss is wedged in thar so tight that Ben had to cut the saddle off, then they ain't no way he's a-gonna git Buster outta thar alive."

Hildy looked at her cousin in alarm. "You think he'll have to be shot?"

"If he can't be rescued," Spud said matter-of-factly. "He can't be allowed to starve to death."

"Then we've got to save him!" Hildy said firmly.

"How ye gonna do that?" Ruby asked.

Hildy didn't know. She watched Ben move the saddle, blanket, and bridle against the base of the cliff and away from the horse. When he reached Hildy, Ruby, and Spud, he was breathing so hard Hildy was frightened.

Ben ignored his symptoms. "Buster's wedged in but I think he could be freed with the help of a couple of men and some equipment. We'll need a saw, ax, pulley, and ropes. Salter will have them. We'll need his help, too."

Hildy frowned. "What about Vernon?"

"Buster has to come first, Hildy," Ben said grimly.

"You mean you'll have to let Vernon escape?"

The old ranger looked at the sky. "I have to get Buster out of here before that next storm hits."

Ruby exclaimed, "But ye said that ketchin' Vernon was mighty important."

Ben nodded. "It is, but saving Buster's life is even more important than clearing my reputation. Let's find that shortcut to Salter's and hope we can still beat Vernon there."

Ben led the way up the talus to the ridge where they had turned off. By then everyone was panting hard.

Hildy anxiously glanced around. "Brother Ben, do you think Vernon's going to ambush us?"

"I don't think so," he panted, "because I don't think he has any idea we're on his trail."

Hildy remembered the mountain lion tracks and the pistol shot. She mentioned these to Ben.

"The lion was probably just curious and followed the horse," Ben said, his breathing ragged. "I have a hunch Vernon spotted the cat and fired to scare it away."

"Would it attack Buster?" Hildy asked.

Ben shook his head. "No ordinary mountain lion would tackle a full-grown horse, but finding one trapped might cause a cat to try. I'd be willing to stay here and protect Buster while you kids went for help. But with Vernon between here and Salter's place I can't let you do that."

*Your health is in danger, too,* Hildy thought, watching the way the old ranger breathed in ragged gulps while beads of perspiration formed on his forehead. Hildy felt her insides tighten as she saw him scout ahead, looking for the landmarks Quint had told him about.

She lowered her voice so only Ruby and Spud could hear. "Brother Ben's pushing himself too hard. Have you noticed how he's perspiring and breathing so loudly?"

"Yeah," Ruby answered. "An' knowin' about his hoss won't make him feel any better."

Hildy added, "None of us whispered when we saw Buster, so Vernon may have heard us and know we're on his trail. He could be waiting to ambush us just as he did Brother Ben so long ago."

"Not if we take the shortcut," Spud replied.

Hildy shot the boy a hopeful glance. "Do you really think so?"

"Absolutely," he assured her. "And time is critical. We've got to beat Vernon to the hermit's place, rescue Buster, and capture Vernon before Ben's strength fails."

As a shadow engulfed them, Hildy glanced at the sky. Wind-driven clouds scudded overhead, filling the canyons with threatening darkness. "Maybe we have another race against the clock," she said thoughtfully.

"Yeah," Ruby observed, squinting at the gathering clouds. "This could be that big one them weather forecasters was talkin' about."

Up ahead, the old ranger turned back and waved them forward. He had found the landmarks. Soon the party was making good time toward the Devil's Backbone. Hildy had no trouble identifying that from a distance. It was a long, blue-gray mountain ridge resembling a giant spine.

The sun was past its zenith when Ben stopped in the shade

of a tall sugar pine. "Lunch," he announced, his voice sounding raspy from his harsh breathing.

Hildy suspected the old ranger stopped more for the need to catch his breath than the need to eat something. She didn't dare share her fears with Ruby or Spud when they sat down on a fallen white pine log beside Ben.

Each one pulled out the sack lunches that Martha Armstrong had prepared. Hildy found a piece of fried chicken, and waited for Ben to return thanks. His face was pale and drawn. *I wonder how much pain he's hiding?* she asked herself. *My own lungs burn from climbing these mountains, and I'm healthy. But cancer is eating his lungs away.*

"Here's the plan," the old ranger said after returning thanks. "When we spot the hermit's place, you kids stay out of sight while I go ahead. I'll call out to Salty so he won't start shooting at me. Quint says he's done that a couple of times when strangers got too close."

Spud swallowed a bite of chicken. "What if Vernon's there ahead of you?"

"I don't think that's possible. Quint says this shortcut will save a lot of travel time—even more, now that Vernon's afoot."

Hildy frowned. "Brother Ben, wouldn't it be better if I went on ahead instead of you? Neither the hermit nor Vernon would be as likely to shoot at a girl."

"Thanks, Hildy," Ben said with a shake of his head, "but I've thought this through pretty carefully. We could use two other men's help in saving Buster. If I could just capture Vernon—"

Ruby almost choked on her food. "I thought ye done give up ketchin' him afore ye rescue yer hoss."

"Saving Buster's my top priority, but I'd get double satisfaction if I could also catch Vernon—" He broke off at a sudden snorting sound.

Hildy dropped her sack and jumped up, whirling around.

A large California black bear with a white triangular mark on his chest stood upright on his hind legs at the edge of a manzanita clump.

"A b'ar!" Ruby gulped, her voice breaking.

"Sit still," Ben said firmly. "He must've stumbled upon us, surprising him as much as us. He'll go away."

Hildy's heart raced until the shaggy animal dropped down on all fours and disappeared into the brush.

Spud said, "I thought bears hibernated all winter."

Ben nodded. "Sows do, but sometimes an old boar will come out in nice weather and look around. The males don't seem to store up as much fat as the females. But that old boy will den up again real soon."

"Do bears eat horses?" Hildy asked.

"Bears eat almost anything. But I'm not half as concerned about a bear or mountain lion bothering Buster as I am about his being caught in a snowstorm."

With that ominous possibility, the party fell silent. When they had finished their meal, they hurried on toward Devil's Backbone. Hildy sensed the urgency that she knew the others also felt, but she was glad when Ben again called a halt at the edge of a dense stand of conifers.

"There's the cabin," he announced quietly, pointing.

Hildy saw that it was no more than a small shack of peeled logs with a plank roof. Smoke drifted up from the stone chimney.

"Everybody look around carefully," the old ranger instructed in a low tone. "Try to spot the hermit if you can." He paused, then added, "And make sure he's alone."

*He means make sure Zane Vernon didn't somehow beat us here,* Hildy told herself. She joined the others in sweeping the area with quick, darting glances. She saw a similarity to the Armstrongs' place in the layout of corrals, barns, and other outbuildings. There was no sign of horses.

"Looks awfully quiet," Hildy whispered.

"That's what worries me," the old ranger said. He took a step forward and stopped behind the trunk of a big sugar pine. "The chimney smoke means somebody's home, but I wish I could see him before he sees us."

Hildy's mind screamed, *Maybe Zane Vernon got here first!* But she didn't say anything.

Suddenly, from behind them came the unmistakable sound of a gun being cocked. A man's voice commanded harshly, "Don't nobody move!"

CHAPTER
SIXTEEN

# THREAT OF A BLIZZARD

Hildy whirled around, her heart beating in sudden alarm. She had never seen a wild man before, but this one holding a double-barrel shotgun might have been one.

Untidy graying-dark hair spilled from beneath his brown stocking cap. Hazel eyes glittered through one of the escaping locks. Tufts of hair curled out of his ears and nose. The man looked as if he hadn't shaved or had a haircut in years. He probably hadn't bathed in almost as long, Hildy decided, wrinkling her nose.

"Mr. Salter?" Ben asked politely.

"Who wants to know?" the stranger growled, slightly shifting the weapon in his hands.

"I'm Ben Strong," the old ranger answered. "Friend of Quint Armstrong. He told us how to find you." He extended his right hand and took a step forward.

The man ignored Ben's outstretched hand. "Why did you want to find me?" he asked, eyes narrowed in suspicion.

"A couple of reasons. First, because deputies chased a cattle rustler into these mountains and Quint's quite sure he's headed here."

"What for?"

"To hide out until he can cross the Nevada border."

The hermit dismissed that information with a casual wave of his left hand. "I eat cattle rustlers for breakfast. Besides, I don't like company, 'specially uninvited. Me 'n' ol' Henrietta here," he patted the gun, "can take care of ourselves."

Hildy almost smiled. For the first time since the hermit had spoken, she felt a slight easing of tension.

"I'm sure you can take care of yourself," Ben agreed. He hadn't moved after the first step. "But I know this man. Name's Zane Vernon. He's more than a rustler. He's an escaped murderer from a Texas prison—and mean."

"Mean? Didn't Quint tell you I'm about as mean an' o'nery as any man alive?"

"I've heard about you," Ben replied in his soft drawl. "Quint tells me you worked for him. Now, if you don't mind, could we go inside before Vernon catches us all out here?"

"Who're the kids?"

"These are my young friends. Hildy Corrigan, Ruby Konning, and Spud Lawler."

Hildy and the others said hi but the hermit only grunted.

"Guess it won't hurt to talk some," he said, lowering the gun. "But don't you all plan on staying long."

Hildy let out a slow, relieved sigh and looked more carefully at the man. He wore high boots, a grimy sheepskin coat, and leather breeches like those still popular from the Great War, which had ended sixteen years before. The breeches fitted snugly at the waist, flared out at the thighs and tapered to a snug fit at the knees. Hildy had heard that horsehide breeches were almost indestructible.

Hildy, Ruby, and Spud dropped back a few paces as Ben and the old man walked together across the meadow. Hildy noticed that there were narrow, split-hoof tracks in the snow, showing that only deer had been in the area.

Ruby whispered, "What d'ye think? Is he not right in the haid?"

"I don't know," Hildy admitted in a low voice.

"He's an ambiguous one," Spud added softly. "I don't know what to make of him. But right now I'm more apprehensive about the danger Vernon poses to all of us."

Hildy glanced at the dense stand of conifers beyond the shack. "He could sneak up close in those trees."

"Then let's keep a-lookin' at them from inside," Ruby suggested.

They crossed the meadow from the east, skirted the corrals, and headed for the cabin. Hildy raised her voice. "Mr. Salter, where are your horses?"

He turned to look back. "Lost them over the years. Last one died last year. I sure do miss them. I was in the cavalry in the war, you know. Always loved horses."

Spud whispered, "Maybe he was shell shocked in the war. Lots of veterans were."

Approaching the cabin with its plank roof, Hildy noticed the lodgepole logs stuck out a foot or more where they were joined at the corners. Cracks between the logs had been well chinked. There was one window to the left of the door. On both sides of that, hides of various small animals had been turned inside out, stretched, and hung out to dry. Rusted tin cans were scattered about, as though Salter had just opened the door and thrown them out. The door itself had been patched with a piece of tin can nailed to the lower left-hand corner.

"Porcupines," Salter explained, catching Hildy's eye. "They like to chew on wood. You'll see the holes they've made in the floor where grease and salt fell from the stove."

The dwelling had no porch, just a flat stone before the door, which had neither handle nor lock. A small hole had been cut in the door where the handle should be. A short stick protruded from that. Salter moved it a couple of inches to the left, activating a wooden bar inside. The door squeaked open.

"Wipe your feet," Salter growled, scraping the mud and

snow off his own boots on a metal strip supported in a block of sturdy wood. "I try to keep a clean floor."

Hildy and Ruby exchanged glances as the men entered through the door, followed by Spud.

Ruby whispered, "How clean do ye reckon a place kin be when porcupines kin git in?"

Hildy shrugged and stopped inside to let her eyes adjust to the gloom. The cabin seemed to consist of one room, roughly twelve feet wide by twice as long, Hildy guessed. She counted four very dirty windows. One window was over an unmade bunk bed that had been built in on the eastern wall.

There was another window on the south wall to Hildy's left and a third on the opposite end of the room. The fourth window on the western wall was to the right of what appeared to be a door leading to a lean-to bedroom. She hadn't seen that from the outside, because it faced the woods.

Salter broke his weapon, ejecting both shells with the peculiar *thunk* sound common to shotguns. He set his weapon by the door, then walked heavily across the wooden floor and set the shells on the table. He struck a match and lit a kerosene lantern hanging from a spike in the far wall.

Hildy glanced around. The place was dirty, cluttered, and smelly. There were no pictures or calendars, but nails had been driven in all four walls. From these hung an assortment of clothes, hats, tools, leather, string, cans, and other items. The stove on the north wall had developed small holes so that little wisps of smoke seeped out. A galvanized water bucket and dipper rested on a small table near the stove. A cane chair with a rawhide bottom stood between the table and stove.

Hildy focused on an untidy mound of what appeared to be sticks. "What's that behind the stove?" she asked.

"Pack rat's nest," Salter answered, dropping his grimy cap on the table beside the shotgun shells.

"Pack rat?" Hildy echoed, her voice faltering.

"They generally won't hurt you," the man assured her from the left side of the stove. He bent under some crude shelves filled with canned goods. He picked up an empty nail keg in one hand and a lug box in the other.

"Over time," Salter added, turning the keg and box upside down, "pack rats can make a nest three feet high and as much across. But watch out they don't trade you a pretty pebble or some other useless thing for anything shiny you have. Ben, if you got any gold teeth, be mighty careful you don't lose them to Adelle."

Ben smiled at the host's attempt at humor. "Adelle?" Ben repeated. "Is that your rat's name?"

"Is now. My wife had it first, but she died." The hermit set the keg and the box on the floor by the single chair. "You girls and Ben take a seat," Salter added. "Spud, you can grab another couple boxes for you 'n' me."

As Spud obeyed, the recluse continued, "I tried to give my wife all she wanted, but she never liked this place, except for the horses. One day shortly after the last one died, she went in the bedroom there and died, too." He motioned toward the lean-to door.

*I couldn't stand to live out here, either,* Hildy thought. *Especially with a strange man like this.*

Salter continued in a soft, sad tone. "Been mighty quiet since then. We never had any kids. Quiet, 'ceptin' for the rat. One time when I was away, runnin' my trapline for a week, Adelle— the rat, that is—came through the hole the porcupine had gnawed in the door. Built her nest before I got back, so I didn't have the heart to throw her out after all that hard work. You folks mind where you step if she goes runnin' across the floor while we're talkin'."

Hildy had seen too many mice to be afraid of them, but she had such a revulsion about rats that she shivered involuntarily. She drew her feet back close to the lug box on which she was sitting and forced her thoughts away from the rodent.

*This is the day my family was to pack,* Hildy thought with sudden emotional pain. *With everything going on here I almost forgot. And I nearly forgot it's almost Christmas too!*

The hermit took one of the lug boxes from Spud and sat down nearest the stove. Hildy and Ruby had taken seats as far from the rat's nest as possible, so Spud and the old ranger sat between them and their host.

Salter asked, "Now, Ben, what's this wild story you were telling me about some killer coming this way?"

Hildy listened absently as Ben explained about why he and the three young visitors were at Quint's when the deputies came. Hildy's eyes flickered around the room while Ben continued with the other incidents that occurred while trailing Vernon and Buster.

Periodically, Hildy glanced at the floor, fearful that the rat might dash across it. In spite of Salter's claim that he liked to keep a clean floor, Hildy noticed that the wooden planks didn't fit snugly, except where dirt had filled in the cracks.

Hildy fought off a shiver. *I'll be glad when we can get out of here. I hope we save Buster and still get home before dark. But what if Vernon shows up?*

Ben finished by telling the other reason they needed his help: that Buster was trapped and abandoned on the narrow trail. He asked if Salter had equipment to help rescue the gelding.

"You shoulda shot the horse," Salter said bluntly. "Sure, I got rope, pulley, and a saw, but we couldn't free him before the blizzard hits."

Hildy stirred uneasily. "Blizzard?" she asked.

Salter nodded. "Might be. Anyway, it's coming up a bad storm. I can always feel it in my bones. So you folks better haul your carcasses outta here and hope you get back to Quint's before it breaks."

Hildy exclaimed, "You mean you won't help save Buster?"

"Look, little lady," the recluse said, "you're strangers who come bustin' into my world without bein' invited. I don't owe you nothin', 'cept my thanks for tellin' me about this Vernon person. I'll take care of him when he comes." Salter stood and added, "So thanks—and goodbye."

Hildy stared in disbelief. Quint had warned about the hermit, but never in her life had Hildy met anyone like him. She exchanged glances with Ruby, Spud, and Ben as they all stood in awkward and uncertain silence.

Ben used his right forefinger to give his white walrus moustache a flip. "Mr. Salter, I'm sorry if we did anything to offend you, but surely you must see—"

Hildy interrupted. "Here comes Vernon!"

Ben turned to look through the west window by the door to the lean-to. "He's running out of the trees toward the house!"

Ben straightened up and spoke crisply. "Hildy, keep an eye on him and tell me whether he heads for the north or south side. Remember, he's armed and dangerous. All of you do exactly what I say; I don't want anyone to get hurt. Hildy, when you see which end of the cabin he chooses, you three get into that lean-to and stay quiet."

"What're you going to do?" Hildy asked anxiously.

"Vernon didn't cross the meadow, so he didn't see our tracks," Ben replied, picking up the rifle Mrs. Armstrong had loaned him. "If he didn't see us come in, he'll only be expecting one person in here. I'm going to slip outside and try to surprise him. Mr. Salter, I'd be obliged if you sat right where you are."

"Now hold on there!" the hermit exclaimed. "I don't hanker to have no stranger tellin' me what to do! You stand back, and when he comes through that door, me 'n' old Henrietta will give him a surprise!"

"No," Ben said firmly, checking the load in his weapon. "I don't want anyone hurt. Please do as—"

Hildy broke in. "He's heading for the south side!"

"Good!" Ben replied. "I'll go to the north. There's no more time for talking." Ben reached for the wooden bar that held the door shut. He lifted the bar quietly and slipped outside.

Hildy wanted to wait until she was sure he had safely reached the north window, but she didn't dare.

"You heard Brother Ben," she said in a hoarse whisper. "Come on, Ruby, Spud."

She plunged through the lean-to door, hearing the hermit

muttering angrily behind her. The tiny room had only one small window in the west side, so Hildy couldn't see well. But she immediately dropped to the floor.

"Get down!" she hissed to Ruby and Spud. "Be quiet!"

As they obeyed, Hildy heard the cabin's outside door crash open.

# Chapter Seventeen

# RACING THE STORM

Hildy's heart thudded so hard it seemed about to burst from her ribs as she crouched on the floor of the lean-to. Ruby and Spud beside her were barely visible in the darkened room. Subconsciously, Hildy was aware of the smells of a woman's colognes or powders in the small bedroom.

Hildy heard Zane Vernon's harsh voice through the closed door. "Drop it, mister!"

"No, you drop yours!" the hermit snapped.

Vernon replied, "You know what, mister? I think you're trying to pull a bluff on me. I see two shotgun shells on the table over there, so I'm guessing you didn't load that thing before you grabbed it."

Salter's voice challenged, "Think so, eh? Well, if you're wrong, you'll never know for sure, because I'm giving you a count of three to drop that gun. One . . ."

Hildy cringed and lowered her face close to the floor, expecting to hear shots.

Instead, she heard the old ranger's voice. "You heard him, Vernon! Drop it!"

Hildy's head jerked up. She glanced hopefully at the closed door, but Spud pulled her down. "Wait!" he whispered.

"Do it now, Vernon!" Ben's voice was sharp and firm.

Hildy swallowed hard, staring at the door.

After what seemed like an awfully long time of total silence, she heard a gun clatter to the floor.

"That's better," Ben said, his tone softening. "Mr. Salter, I'd be obliged if you'd pick up his pistol. Then find something to tie him with."

Hildy took a quick deep breath and turned to grin happily at Ruby and Spud. They leaped up and opened the door to the main cabin.

Vernon faced the eastern wall while the old ranger quickly searched him. The rustler was dressed much as he had been the first time Hildy had seen him stealing Ben's livestock, except he hadn't shaved for days. Salter pulled a coil of rope from the south wall as Hildy, Ruby, and Spud stood in the doorway of the lean-to.

"You got him!" Hildy exclaimed. "You got him!"

The old ranger didn't answer, but took the rope from the recluse and tied Vernon's hands behind his back.

He demanded of Ben, "How come you know my name? Who in blazes are you? And why're you doing this to me?"

Ben continued tying the ropes. "My name's Ben Strong, and I'm making a citizen's arrest for murder, resisting arrest, unlawful flight, escape from prison, cattle rustling, and horse stealing."

Vernon opened his mouth as if to make some angry remark, but paused as Hildy, Ruby, and Spud came closer to him. He frowned at Hildy. "Don't I know you?"

She didn't answer as Ben finished his task and stepped back. "Move to that chair," he ordered, pointing.

The recluse followed the prisoner and his captor across the room. "Ben," Salter said ruefully, "it's been a long time since I was so glad to see somebody come through that door like you just did."

"Sometimes we need each other, Mr. Salter."

"Call me Salty. You saved my bacon when I got caught with an empty gun. When you're ready to try saving your horse, I'd be proud to help."

Hildy started to smile in approval, but Vernon scowled at Ben. "Horse? You mean that spavined old nag I rode up here is yours?"

"Careful how you speak of Buster," the old ranger replied softly. "Sit down and stay there."

Vernon obeyed, easing into the rawhide-bottom chair, hands behind his back. "You look vaguely familiar," he said to the old ranger. "And how come you're making all those charges against me?"

"There'll be time for explanations later, Vernon." Ben turned to the recluse. "Salty, I'd appreciate your showing me where I can find a saw, more rope, a pulley, and anything else we might need to save Buster before it gets too dark to see or the storm breaks."

"Got some one-inch cotton rope in the shed," the hermit replied. "I'll get it and the other things."

A short time later he returned with a trapper's ax, pruning saw, a pulley and rope. Hildy stepped outside with the others, then blinked in surprise. The sky was completely overcast and threatening.

Vernon complained, "Any fool can see a storm's coming. Why're you forcing me out in weather like this to watch you try saving a worthless old horse?"

"You're not going to watch," Ben said evenly, motioning for the prisoner to walk ahead of him. "You got Buster into that mess. You're going to help get him out."

"The blazes I am," Vernon growled. "You can't make me lift a hand."

Ben didn't answer, but Salter cautioned, "If I was you, mister, I'd be mighty careful about slipping and falling into that canyon. It's a powerful long way down."

"You threatening me?" Vernon demanded.

"I know the area," Salter replied. "I was just offering a little friendly advice."

At the top of the ravine where Ben had stopped to rest before, Ben called a halt. Hildy heard his ragged, uneven breathing as he stood, with Vernon in front of him.

"You all right, Brother Ben?" Hildy asked quietly, slipping up beside him.

His voice was so low Hildy had to strain to catch the words. "I'll make it." He turned to Salter and Vernon. "The way I figure it, Salty, we can saw down a stout tree and use the trunk as a pry bar." He paused, panting hard, before continuing. "Then we can tie the pulley to that white fir, run your rope though it twice for strength, and take the other end down to my horse."

The recluse nodded as Ben continued, "Then we make a collar with the rope to go around his neck. Maybe run a short lead rope from the bridle off to the right so somebody can pull on it and keep the horse's head uphill. We need all the weight we can get on that side to keep him from going into the canyon when we pry him out of there."

Ben pointed. "We'll have to climb up on that boulder and ease the timber straight down between the rock and Buster's left side. Then we swing the other end of the timber back this way, making the front end go under his belly.

"We rest the bar across the boulder as a fulcrum while some-body pries down on this end of the timber. As the horse is forced up, we use the pulley to keep him from sliding back. Eventually, he'll come up out of there and straight back."

Hildy protested, "You mean you'll tip him completely over backward?"

Vernon chuckled. "That's what he means. But that trail's so narrow you'll be lucky if the horse doesn't roll right into the canyon. And with the slippery snow and the slick shale under-foot, you'd better figure on some of you going over the side with him."

"That's enough, Vernon," Ben said.

The man didn't seem to hear. "But that's the only way it can be done. When I dismounted and tried to lead him through there and he got caught, I tried everything I could think of to get him to back up. I coaxed and cussed and yelled at him, hit him with my hat, but he wouldn't back. Finally, I even stuck him in the shoulder with the end of my knife, but—"

"You didn't!" Hildy cried in disbelief.

Vernon smiled without humor. "Not very deep."

"How could you do something so cruel to a defenseless horse?" Hildy retorted hotly.

"He wasn't exactly defenseless, little lady. Fact is, he tried to bite me. But then, when he wouldn't back up, I knew he couldn't get loose."

Ruby cried indignantly, "So you jist left him thar to die! Well, I hope when they put you back in prison this time, they put ye where ye cain't never escape!"

Vernon glowered at her. "How'd you know I was in prison?"

"Never mind!" Ben broke in. "There's no time to talk. Mr. Salter, do you want to cut a timber or set up the pulley?"

"I'll fix the pulley."

Spud volunteered, "Designate which tree you want, Ben. I'll saw it down and trim the branches off while you make a collar for Buster."

Ben looked around. "Find one about as big around as my leg." He pointed. "Like that lodgepole pine. See it?"

The boy nodded. He hurried off with the saw and ax. The hermit carried the rope and pulley to the white fir.

Hildy asked, "Brother Ben, what can Ruby and I do?"

"Tie Vernon's legs with about three feet of rope so he can hobble but not run." Ben handed her a short length of rope and looked at the prisoner. "Not that I expect you to make the mistake of trying to escape again."

"Again?" Vernon asked.

The old ranger didn't answer. He turned and eased his way across the shale, carrying the rifle and one end of the long cotton rope. Hildy bent to tie the prisoner's legs while Ruby kept an eye on him.

"What'd he mean, *again*?" Vernon repeated.

Hildy didn't reply because Ben hadn't. She guessed that was because of the painful memories Ben had of his prisoner escaping and ambushing him years before.

"I don't know that old duffer, but now I remember where I've seen you before," Vernon said as Hildy finished her task and stood up. "How come you're way out here with that old man?"

"Ask him," Hildy answered evasively, stepping back.

The prisoner stared thoughtfully at the old ranger's back. "Say, he reminds me a little . . . Naw, can't be."

"Could be," Ruby teased.

Vernon twisted his head to more thoroughly study Ben. "I remember a long drink of water like him back in Texas, but that was many years ago." He shook his head. "Couldn't be."

"Ye know that for shore?" Ruby asked.

Hildy gave her cousin a warning look, but Ruby didn't seem to notice. "Ye kilt his daddy!" she blurted. "Ben was a Texas Ranger. He caught ye, but ye excaped an' ambushed him. Ye left him for daid, but his hoss saved him. That's the same man, same hoss."

Vernon exclaimed, "No, I can't believe that!"

"Ye better believe it," Ruby said firmly.

Hildy took Ruby's arm. "Let's go help."

"Wait!" Vernon said. When the girls turned, he jerked his head toward Ben. "That old man mean a lot to you two?"

They nodded but said nothing.

Vernon's eyes narrowed and his voice grew cold. "Then you'd better help me escape."

"What?" Hildy almost sputtered.

"Oh, I'll get away by myself before we all get back to civilization," Vernon assured her, keeping his voice low. "But if you help me, I won't hurt him this time."

Ruby flared, "Why ye ol' hornytoad! If'n ye so much as lay a hand on him, I'll snatch ye plumb baldheaded!"

"Easy, Ruby," Hildy urged, seizing her cousin's arm and

turning her away from Vernon. "Let's go."

The girls again headed toward the old ranger, but Vernon's voice followed. It was loud enough for them to hear, but not Spud or the two men.

"If you two help me, I'll be nice to the others, including that freckle-faced boy and the both of you. Otherwise . . ." Vernon's words trailed off into an ominous, unspoken threat.

"Reckon he means it?" Ruby whispered to Hildy as they approached the shale.

Hildy shivered. "Yes, he means it."

At the beginning of the shale, standing on the narrow trail below the cliff, Hildy carefully peered over the canyon rim. *After what Vernon did, I'm glad Brother Ben caught him. But we're a long way from help. If Vernon escapes out here, we could all end up at the bottom of this canyon.*

Hildy glanced up at the dark sky just as the first snowflakes touched her face. She fought a sickening feeling inside as her thoughts jumped back to her family.

"Ruby, I hope our folks aren't worried about us."

"I reckon muh daddy is startin' to do some powerful prayin' right about now."

"I was supposed to help my family move today."

"I know. I've been thinkin' about that. I'm sorry they're movin', and also sorry about us bein' out here with that turrible man at a time like this."

"Me too."

The snow fell faster. Spud came hurrying down, carrying the saw and dragging a freshly cut lodgepole pine. "Sure getting dark fast," he remarked.

The hermit called from the tree where he'd attached the pulley, "It's no use, Ben! Better leave everything and skedaddle outta here before it snows so hard we can't find our way back to the cabin!"

Hildy glanced at the old ranger, who squinted at the sky, then at Buster. His Adam's apple bobbed and he sighed deeply, as if in pain. His chin dropped momentarily. Then resolutely, as though facing a problem over which he had no control, he raised his head. He turned to face the girls. "I sure hate to leave him, but . . ." He paused, then added, "Better untie Vernon's ankles."

Hildy protested, "But Buster'll die if we leave him out here now!"

Vernon replied, "So will we if we don't get back to the cabin. Untie my ankles like he said."

As the girls reluctantly approached Vernon, he asked, "You two ever been snowbound?"

"Never," Ruby admitted as Hildy stooped to undo the prisoner's ankle ropes.

"Some terrible things can happen when people are snowbound in a little cabin," Vernon said in a low, ominous voice. "Sometimes only one person leaves there alive."

"Ye cain't skeer us!" Ruby scoffed.

"Can't I?" Vernon seemed to purr with menacing satisfaction. "Well, before this storm's over, you're all going to be more than scared. Take my word for it!"

—

# CHAPTER EIGHTEEN

# A PERILOUS RESCUE ATTEMPT

After the hermit made a supper of canned beans fried in bacon grease, he worked out sleeping accommodations. He offered to give up his single bunk to Ben, but the old ranger refused. He'd slept on the ground many a time, Ben explained. The cabin floor would be fine. Spud said he'd slept in boxcars and in hobo jungles. He'd also be comfortable on the floor.

Ben allowed Vernon's hands to be retied in front, but his ankles were secured to the kitchen stove with a short length of rope. Even so, Hildy had some anxious moments as she remembered Vernon's threats.

Salter told the girls, "You can have the lean-to bed." He left Spud, Ben, and Vernon with the kerosene lantern. Salter lit a match and used its flaring light to lead the girls into the lean-to. He lit a lamp, and for the first time, Hildy saw clearly where she, Ruby, and Spud had taken refuge earlier that day.

A double bed and dresser had been crammed into the tiny room. A box of powder and a bottle of cologne were on the dresser in front of the mirror. Old calendar pictures decorated the walls. Curtains graced the window.

"I built this room for my wife," the hermit explained, holding the light high. "After she died, I closed it off and almost never come in here anymore."

Hildy was touched by the signs of gentleness in the man who had spoken so bluntly earlier.

He placed the lamp on the dresser. "She made the quilts herself; you'll sleep warm. I'll close the door so the rat won't bother you. Don't worry about that man."

"We won't," Ruby answered, but Hildy said nothing.

The cousins thanked their host, who left, closing the door after him. The girls undressed quickly down to their homemade underwear in the unheated room, and slid into bed.

Hildy blew out the lamp, then prayed silently: *Lord, please protect us from that awful man. And get us back to our families in time for Christmas.*

Ruby asked, "You think Vernon meant what he said 'bout excapin', and only one person leaving this place alive? Or was he jist tryin' to skeer us?"

"I'm afraid he meant it."

"Well, he'd be a fool to try anything during this storm 'cause he couldn't git away. Reckon Ben an' Mr. Salter think the same thing, 'cause I hear 'em snorin'. Don't rightly see how they kin sleep, knowin' they's a convicted murderer in that room. Plus a pack rat."

"I've prayed for the Lord's protection, so go to sleep."

"I'm skeered that Vernon's jist bidin' his time, and maybe tonight's the night."

"You need to have faith, Ruby."

"I never held much with faith," she admitted ruefully. "But they ain't much other choice."

Hildy didn't answer, and silence settled until Ruby asked, "Ye reckon—I mean—do you think Glenn noticed my trying to talk better—at least around him?"

Hildy smiled in the darkness. "I'm sure of it."

In spite of her concerns, Hildy finally slept. She had unpleasant dreams about her family—not knowing if she was alive or dead. She dreamed it was after Christmas before she got out of the mountains, and she couldn't find her family. Then in her dream she saw Vernon had escaped and was smiling evilly at her.

"See?" he said, reaching for her. "I told you—"

Ruby awakened her. "Yo're a-talkin' in yore sleep, Hildy. Anyway, it's time to git up."

Hildy sat up, anxiously glancing out the window. She was relieved to see that the snow seemed to be stopping.

"I doubt that it's safe to risk trying to walk all the way back to the Armstrongs' until we're sure this storm is over," Hildy said. "But I sure hope it is."

"I jist hope we git outta here alive. That Vernon skeers me," Ruby said as she hurriedly dressed.

When the cousins entered the main cabin, the hermit turned from the stove and nodded to the girls. Spud smiled at them. Ben and Vernon were just coming in from outside.

"Face it," Vernon was saying. "Your horse most likely froze to death last night. There's no sense even going to check on him."

"I don't think the temperature quite got down to freezing," Ben replied. "Besides, Buster's trapped under a south-facing cliff, so he might've stayed warmer."

Spud said, "I'll go with you to check, Ben."

"We'll all go," the hermit replied.

Although Hildy was eager to get home, she recognized from the threatening sky that the storm might not be over. She was also anxious to see how Buster had fared. However, she was uneasy because walking through more new snow would undoubtedly be hard on Ben. It would also be easier for Vernon to try escaping while everyone was concentrating on rescuing Buster.

After a breakfast of bacon cut from the rind, biscuits and country gravy, the six left the cabin. The old ranger set a slower pace than yesterday, Hildy noticed. He also stopped frequently, apparently with the intention of examining signs in the snow, but Hildy suspected he was hurting. He certainly was having greater trouble breathing than before.

Vernon, his hands tied in front of him but without his ankle hobbles, seemed to delight in making cruel remarks to his captor. As they started on again, he turned to the old ranger walking behind him. "You're on a fool's errand, Ben. First of all, you can see this weather's not going to hold. It'll start storming again and catch us out in the open. And even if we get to that fool horse before the storm breaks, we've no food or water for him. He may have licked at the snow, but most likely he's dead."

When Ben didn't reply, the prisoner tried again: "You know that mountain lions love horseflesh. So do bears. They might be hibernating, but not the lions. Like the one I shot at. If he finds that helpless horse—"

"That's enough!" Ben said sharply.

He spoke with such authority that Vernon fell silent. He remained that way until they reached the ridge above the horse. Walking ahead of the others, Vernon stopped abruptly and pointed. "That big cat's back. I bet he had horse for breakfast."

"Oh, be quiet!" Hildy snapped, hurrying ahead to where she could look down the talus. Her heart sank at the sight of Buster. He was still wedged between the boulder and the cliff, but was not moving.

*He's dead!* she thought.

Ben came up beside Hildy and whistled shrilly. Buster jerked his head up and whinnied weakly.

"He's alive!" Hildy cried. "He's alive!"

As the party approached, everyone but the prisoner commented excitedly. Hildy saw that the gelding's left hind shoe was badly worn from striking his hoof futilely against the boulder.

Hildy's mittened hand flew to her mouth as Buster whinnied again and tried to turn his head toward his master. "Oh!" Hildy moaned, seeing blood between Buster's forehead and his right ear. "He's hurt himself swinging his head against the cliff." She fought back the tears.

Ben turned to the hermit and handed him the rifle. "Hold this, please. Everyone stay here."

Salter accepted the rifle, holding it awkwardly with the shotgun while Ben eased down toward the horse.

Hildy put her arms around Ruby and waited, but even from beyond the shale, now buried under new snow, Hildy could see that Buster had other terrible wounds.

Spud came close to the girls and spoke softly to them.

Hildy nodded, still struggling to keep from crying.

Ben completed his inspection and came back, breathing with difficulty. "He's tried so hard to free himself that his right front shoe's almost worn off. The side of that hoof is starting to wear down from striking it against the cliff. The left hind hoof is worn almost to the bone. He's rubbed the hair off his jawbone, and he's got a hole in his head."

Hildy felt sick. "What're you going to do?"

Without a word, the old ranger turned to Salter and retrieved the rifle. Then he started down the trail again toward the horse.

Tears flooded Hildy's eyes, and she wanted to turn away, but she couldn't.

She watched as Ben stopped at end of the boulder by Buster's left side. Slowly, the old ranger raised the rifle. Hildy turned away.

She heard him say softly, "I'm sorry, old partner."

Hildy and Ruby, with arms entwined flinched at the sound of the rifle bolt being drawn back to full cock position. Hildy held her breath, her back to the tragic drama.

But their was no shot. Slowly, Hildy forced herself to look at Ben and Buster again.

Buster whinnied, his wide eyes focused on his owner in silent expectation. Ben slowly lowered the rifle. Quietly, he turned and retraced his steps.

"He sure wants to live," the old ranger said in his soft drawl. "And he certainly doesn't expect to die by the hands of a friend.

Let's see if we can't get him out of there before the storm chases us out again."

With glad cries from Hildy, Ruby, and Spud, everyone eased down the slope while the old ranger assigned duties.

"Spud, dig around in the snow and see if you can find that timber you cut yesterday. Ruby, I'd be obliged if you could run the rope back from the pulley when Mr. Salter feeds it through. Hildy, I'd like your help in getting the other end of the rope around Buster's neck as a collar. Vernon, we can use your weight on the timber when we try prying Buster out of there."

"I can't do that with my hands tied," Vernon protested. "I'm liable to slip into the canyon."

Ben hesitated. "I want you alive for trial, Vernon. Hildy, untie him, please."

She wanted to protest, but the old ranger turned away. Hildy reluctantly began working on the rope knots. She said, "I hope you understand that means he's trusting you not to try escaping."

Vernon almost chuckled. "Oh, he can trust me. You can all trust me—for now!"

The chilling threat sent goose bumps rippling up and down Hildy's arms.

Hildy estimated about an hour had passed before everything was in place for trying to rescue Buster. The sky had grown ominously dark, and there was a dead calm when she and the old ranger completed a collar from the one-inch cotton rope. This ran from the horse's withers, along the back and rump. Hildy passed the rope to the end of the boulder, where Vernon took it. He gingerly eased across the snow that hid the loose shale. Beyond that point, Ruby took the rope up to the hermit. He ran the rope twice through the pulley, which he had secured against the trunk of a towering white fir.

The front end of the twelve-foot section of lodgepole pine Spud had sawed down and trimmed of branches was in place under Buster's body. The pole's center rested on the back end of the boulder, waiting for weight to be applied there.

"I think we're ready," Ben announced. "Soon's we all catch our breath."

Ruby looked apprehensively at the sky. "It's a . . . startin' to snow again," she said nervously.

"It's just spitting," the hermit replied. "But you can bet your bottom dollar it'll get worse."

*Dollar!* Hildy's thoughts leaped back to her family. *If we get home in time, and if Daddy could repay my silver dollar that I loaned him, I'd just barely have time to buy a gift for Molly to put in that red box.*

Ben interrupted her thoughts. "Let's try it. Salty, if you put your weapon down, you can use both hands to take up the slack with the pulley when we pry Buster up. Vernon, your weight is needed down here with Spud and me on the end of this pole. Ruby, help with the pulley rope. Hildy, I put a lead rope through Buster's bridle. If you'll take the end of that rope and stand over there by the cliff, you can keep Buster's head drawn toward you. Now, let's do it."

When everyone was in place, Ben's voice came clearly across the mountain stillness. "On the count of three. One, two . . ."

*Oh, Lord!* Hildy closed her eyes and prayed silently, holding onto Buster's lead rope. *Don't let them slip and fall backward into that canyon!*

"Three!" Ben's voice made Hildy open her eyes.

Spud, Ben, and Vernon threw their weight down hard on the loose end of the timber, using the boulder as the fulcrum for their lever. Hildy tensed her muscles, joining them in spirit.

Ruby let out a joyous whoop from where she and the recluse held the pulley rope by the fir tree. "I think ye done moved him up a mite!"

"Don't talk!" the hermit interrupted. "If we get the least little bit of slack, help me pull—"

He broke off as the timber suddenly slipped from under the horse. The lever, released of its tension, leaped into the air like a living thing, throwing Spud, Ben, and Vernon off balance.

"Oh, no!" the words exploded from Hildy as she watched helplessly.

Ben, Spud, and Vernon, flailing their arms frantically, slid on the shale and snow, falling backward toward the canyon's edge!

# CHAPTER NINETEEN

# SNOWBOUND AND CABIN FEVER

Hildy dropped Buster's lead rope and screamed. Her cry seemed to echo. Then she vaguely knew Ruby had also shrieked as Spud, Ben, and Vernon slid backward toward the cliff's edge.

As Hildy watched in helpless horror, she saw Spud grab frantically for the end of the great boulder that held Buster captive. The boy's fingers slid, then caught and held in a crevice. With his other hand, he snagged the old ranger's arm. He swung his booted feet away from the canyon's edge. Vernon's feet shot out over the edge before he managed to grab a young evergreen sapling.

Hildy dashed recklessly across the treacherous shale to the boulder. She held on to it with one hand and reached the other out to Spud. When he regained his feet, they helped the old ranger and Vernon to safety.

By then, Ruby and the hermit were there too. They all stood panting in the mountain air, their eyes drawn to the tangle of huge jagged boulders far below the canyon's rim.

"Thank God!" Hildy exclaimed when she could find her voice. "For a moment there, I thought—"

"Me too," Ben broke in, still breathing hard. "Well, it's too risky trying that again in this worsening weather. We'd better head for cover and try again later."

Hildy knew it was a major defeat, because no other rescue attempt could be made today, and by tomorrow, Buster might be dead. Aching with disappointment, she joined the others in the silent retreat to the cabin.

Snow was falling in wide, feathery flakes when they opened the door and clomped inside. While Ben tied Vernon's ankles with ropes, the hermit said, "Looks like it's going to storm enough for us to be snowbound for a spell, so we may's well be comfortable. I'll rassle us up some lunch."

Hildy wanted to keep her mind off their disappointing situation, her longing for home, and the dangers facing them, especially from Vernon. She asked, "May Ruby and I do that, Mr. Salter?"

He gave her a hard look. "You think I can't make something fit to eat?"

Hildy was taken aback at the man's harsh tone. She caught Vernon's eye and recalled his warning about what could happen when people were trapped in a cabin because of bad weather. Hildy tried to sound reassuring. "Oh no, of course not, Mr. Salter! But we're used to cooking and I—"

He interrupted with a grunt. "Guess I could take a day off. Grab one of them airtights off that shelf."

Hildy and Ruby looked at each other without understanding, then at the hermit.

"Airtights?" Hildy asked.

"Canned food!" he snapped, pointing to a shelf lined with shiny cans. "They're called airtights." He walked away, muttering under his breath.

Hildy and Ruby looked at each other, then grinned.

"Anybody play cards?" the recluse asked, sitting on the edge of his bunk bed. He motioned for Spud, Ben, and Vernon to draw up seats and sit down.

Hildy heard Vernon say that he played, but Ben and Spud said they didn't.

Salter declared, "It's no fun with only two players. How about talking? Everybody tell where they come from. Spud, you first."

Hildy wanted to listen, but her focus was on the meager selection of canned goods. *Beans!* she thought with distaste. *Pork and beans. Green beans. There's nothing but beans.*

Carefully, she opened a small closed cupboard under the shelves, hoping the rat wouldn't pop out at her. She gave a small sigh of relief when she saw only a slab of bacon with the rind and an open can of pure lard. She closed the cupboard door and took a large can of pork and beans from the shelf.

Ruby rummaged in a drawer of flatware for a can opener. "I reckon Mr. Salter's gittin' a little short-tempered," she said, so softly only Hildy could hear. "Do you suppose that's because he's not used to company, or because he's gittin' cabin fever?"

Hildy rubbed the top of the can with a dish towel, then held it for Ruby to open. "I wouldn't choose him or Zane Vernon to be snowbound with."

"That's for shore!" Ruby inserted the point of the can opener in the shiny top. "We know Vernon's a bad man, but we don't know nothin' 'bout Mr. Salter, 'ceptin' he's got some reason fer livin' out here all by hisself. Fer all we know, he could be wanted for murder, too."

"I hadn't thought of that," Hildy admitted, glancing anxiously toward the men. "It doesn't ease my mind any about what could happen to us away out here in this isolated cabin."

Ruby whispered, "Did ye see this skillet? An' the dishes? In the daylight, I kin see that they're downright dirty! I'm a-gonna boil some water an' wash 'em real good before usin' 'em."

"Just don't make him mad," Hildy warned as Ruby finished opening the can of beans. "If he says anything, tell him we're used to working, and we like to keep busy."

"I'd like to be out of here," Ruby replied sourly.

"Me too." Hildy glanced around the room. "There's no calendar here, but Tuesday is Christmas."

"Well, they ain't no sign of Christmas hereabouts."

Hildy brightened. "Then let's make some." She turned to Spud and the three men. "How about singing Christmas carols?" she asked cheerfully.

Spud and Ben nodded, but Vernon and Salter stared at her in disbelief.

"Ruby and I'll start," Hildy offered. "How about 'O Little Town of Bethlehem'?" She swung the can opener in a down beat and began singing with her cousin. Spud and the old ranger immediately followed. A moment later, the other two men started singing tentatively.

By the time they reached "Silent Night," a change had come over everyone. Lunch was ready, and they pulled up their makeshift seats and sat down in silence around the small table.

Impulsively, Hildy asked, "Mr. Salter, would it be all right with you if we returned thanks?"

He blinked at her. "Return thanks?"

"Yes. I'm sure Brother Ben wouldn't mind saying grace for all of us."

The hermit hesitated, his eyes slowly softening. "Nobody's done that in this house since my wife died," he said thoughtfully. "Jist like there's not been a Christmas song around here in years. Ben, would you?"

Hildy smiled her gratitude, closed her eyes and bowed her head.

The old ranger's soft drawling voice filled the tiny cabin. "Lord, as we approach this most sacred season of the year, we praise Thee for bringing us together in safety in a time of storm. We thank Thee for Mr. Salter's kindness in sharing his home and his food. We ask Thee to bless the food and multiply it back to our host.

"We ask Thee to be with our families and friends, who must be worrying greatly about us. Give them Thy peace, and let us all soon return safely to our families. Bring us together for Christmas, so we may all rejoice in the wonder and joy of Thy Son's birthday.

"We also ask Thy guidance upon us as we seek to save a noble horse from an ignoble death. Most of all, we thank Thee for the gift of the Baby who was born so long ago that through Him we all can live for Thy glory here on earth and spend eternity with Thee."

When Ben said a soft "Amen," Hildy heard it echoed around the table. Startled, she lifted her eyes, wondering if she'd heard correctly. The hermit's eyes were bright, and Hildy was sure he'd been moved. But she looked into the prisoner's eyes and couldn't be certain. Had he softened or was he still a threat to their lives?

The question still bothered Hildy the next morning when she awoke to see that it was snowing harder.

Ruby joined Hildy in looking out the lean-to window at the snowflakes swirling down, covering everything with a pristine mantle of white. "They ain't no way we can help Buster today, and we don't dare try walking back to the Armstrongs'."

"It's Sunday," Hildy replied. "Two days before Christmas. We can't go to church, but maybe we can at least have some kind of service right here."

Ruby shook her head. "I ain't never been in church with a murderer before."

"We've never been snowbound before either. So let's get dressed and see if Brother Ben'll help us honor the Lord's Day."

Before she could speak privately to the old ranger, Hildy noticed the change that began in everyone last night continued in all but Vernon. He was silent and remote, his eyes alert. The others engaged in cheerful conversation.

At breakfast, after Ben again returned thanks, Hildy and Ruby cheerfully did the dishes and thoroughly scrubbed everything in sight. This required their host to bring buckets of snow to be melted on the stove for boiling water.

As the cousins finished and hung their dish cloths and towels to dry, the recluse said, "Hey girls, come join us. Spud's told us all about his background, and I told mine, but Ben and Vernon won't talk. So it's your turn."

"I'd like to have listened to your story, Mr. Salter," Hildy said as she and Ruby joined the circle around the table. "But it was hard to hear because Ruby and I were rattling those pots and pans."

Salter said softly, "I just told how those songs and Ben's prayer brought back memories of my mother, and how I took some wrong turns. Ended up here, with neither kith nor kin."

He paused while a thoughtful silence fell over everyone. The recluse finally cleared his throat and looked at Ruby. "You ready?" he asked.

Ruby nodded, took a deep breath, and started recalling her early life. Hildy was familiar with the story, because the cousins had known each other since childhood. Still, Hildy felt a tinge of sadness as Ruby talked about growing up with a cantankerous grandmother who led her to believe that she was an orphan. Only recently, Ruby reported, had she learned that her father was alive. She told how she, Hildy, and Spud had found him, and now they all lived in Lone River. "Your turn," she said to Hildy.

Hildy shook her head. "I . . . I'd rather not."

The others coaxed, but Hildy demurred.

Vernon volunteered with a smirk, "I'll tell about how Ben and me met years ago."

Hildy glanced at the old ranger and saw the pain in his eyes. She knew he still hurt too much to admit to a stranger like Salter how he had once let a prisoner escape, been ambushed, and would have died if it hadn't been for the horse that they had vainly tried to save.

The irony of it all fascinated Hildy, for after all these years, the two men now sat side by side in a snowbound cabin. But the drama wasn't over—not yet.

"Okay," Hildy said, "I'll tell about myself, but leave Brother Ben alone."

She told about being born in a sharecropper's cabin, of picking cotton when she was five, of the family moving from place to place as her father sought work. Hildy included the story of her mother's death, and of her own promise to her grieving sisters of a "forever" home where they would never again have to move.

She told about finding her faith in God during an Oklahoma lightning storm, and coming to California, and how she dreamed of becoming a teacher. Finally, Hildy told about her family having to move to Flatsville and how much she hated to leave her friends in Lone River.

Hildy concluded, "So I'm sad inside, not just because of having to leave behind the people I love, but because it's the end of something very special."

She looked across the table, her eyes gently resting on each person as she continued: "I guess this is the last adventure I'll have with Ruby, Spud, and Brother Ben. That makes me very, very sad."

Another hush had fallen on everyone when Hildy finished. The snow-filled sky made the cabin's interior so dark that Salter had lit the lantern. He removed it from its nail on the wall and placed it in the center of the table. In the silence, Hildy could hear the faint flicker of the flame as it danced inside the smoky glass chimney.

Finally the recluse spoke, his voice husky. "Hildy, everybody and everything changes. Kids go to school, change grades, and sometimes they even change schools. People move away or die. Since nothing remains the same, we all have to accept change.

"For you, that means moving to Flatsville. But you don't have to give up the dreams you told us about. You can someday make them come true, no matter where you live in the meantime."

The hermit paused and looked around uncomfortably. He added, "Guess I've said enough. But Hildy, I hope you'll learn to accept what life brings, including change."

Hildy was so troubled and thoughtful she barely heard anything else that was said the rest of the day. Even Ruby and Spud seemed to sense her need to be alone with her thoughts. They left her standing at the window, staring out at the falling snow. After a while she closed her eyes.

*O Lord,* she prayed, *so many strange things have happened these last few days. Help me to understand what Thy will is for my life—now.*

She was aroused from her thoughts, hearing Vernon shuffle closeby. She looked out the corner of her eye as he passed behind her and stopped at the table, his ankles still roped together.

Using the long-handled dipper, he brought a drink of water to his lips. He didn't look up, but spoke to Hildy across the dipper, his voice low enough that only she could hear.

"Some things change," he said with such venom that Hildy was startled. "But some things repeat themselves. I'm not going to let that old man take me back to prison for something that happened years ago."

Vernon paused, then hissed, "So if you won't help me escape, let me repeat my warning: I wouldn't count on any of you being home for Christmas."

He turned and hobbled away, leaving Hildy standing in awe, her heart beating wildly against her ribs.

# CHAPTER TWENTY

# The Outlaw's Threat

B adly frightened, Hildy anxiously sought a chance to tell the old ranger of the prisoner's threat. But she had no opportunity to do that because Vernon seemed to deliberately stay close to her all during the evening.

He sat at the table while the girls did the dishes. Hildy sensed his hard, cold eyes on her back so that she didn't even feel like talking with Ruby. Hildy kept a wary eye out for Adelle, the pack rat, but neither that nor Vernon's threat kept Hildy from thinking about her family and Christmas.

Unaware of Vernon's latest threat, Ruby kept trying to listen as Spud, Ben, and the hermit sat at the far end of the cabin telling stories. Hildy's own attention finally shifted there only when she heard the old ranger mention fighting in the Civil War.

She was eager to hear more because he rarely talked about himself. She was hopeful he would also tell about his days as a U.S. Marshal and Texas Ranger. But Hildy was so unnerved by

Vernon's proximity and repeated threats that she couldn't concentrate on Ben's soft voice.

Ruby finally hung her dish towel on a nail and hurried to join the male circle. Hildy quickly placed the heavy iron skillet on its nail by the stove so she could get away from Vernon.

She heard his low voice behind her. "If you help me escape, I'll let you get home."

She whirled around. "No! I couldn't do that!" She dashed across the room to join the others. Her sudden action startled Ruby, Spud, Ben, and Salter. They looked sharply at her.

"Something wrong?" the old ranger asked, glancing suspiciously from her to the prisoner still at the table.

Hildy was tempted to blurt out the truth, but didn't feel that would be wise to do in front of Vernon. He would surely deny the charges, probably start an argument and make matters worse. "It's okay . . ." She looked at the hermit and changed the subject. "What do you want me to do with those tin cans? They're starting to pile up."

"Burn them in the stove," he said. "Getting rid of the food smell keeps animals from messing with the cans after I throw them out. And burning helps them rust faster."

Hildy turned back toward the stove, but Spud volunteered to burn the cans so she could listen to Ben. Hildy joined Ruby and Salter by sitting on an upturned nail keg facing the old ranger.

He spoke in his slow, easy drawl, jumping about chronologically as he recalled certain incidents from his past. Hildy especially liked his telling about being so poor he was barefooted when he participated in the 1889 opening of the Cherokee Strip in Oklahoma Territory. He explained, "It was the biggest horse race in the world."

Spud finished poking tin cans into the stove and rejoined the circle as Ben recalled repairing roads for a dollar a day so he could pay the poll tax in order to vote. But he never mentioned being ambushed by Vernon.

When the prisoner shuffled over with bound ankles to join

the group, Ben fell silent. Vernon did not look at Hildy directly, but she felt as threatened as she would had a coiled rattlesnake been at her feet ready to strike.

Fearful that Vernon would volunteer his version of that long-ago encounter with the old ranger, Hildy impulsively suggested they read the biblical account of Jesus' birth. "Mr. Salter, could we borrow your Bible?"

"Don't have one," he admitted, "but maybe I could recite it from memory."

Hildy and the others exchanged surprised looks as the recluse closed his eyes, paused, then began in a subdued tone. "And it came to pass in those days . . ."

The hermit's voice built in volume, then dropped to a subdued finale. ". . . And suddenly there was with the angel a multitude of heavenly hosts praising God, and saying, 'Glory to God in the highest, and on earth peace, good will toward men.' "

A reverent hush settled over the cabin. Hildy looked sharply at Vernon, but he alone seemed unaffected. He just stared at the ceiling, showing no emotion.

Ruby finally said with awe, "Mr. Salter, that was powerful good! How come ye kin recite like that?"

"I had a saintly mother who taught me a lot when I was little, including how to memorize long passages of scripture." Then he fell silent, obviously unwilling to shed any more light on the very personal part of his life that had taken him from a rich spiritual heritage to what he had become.

He stood up and brought in the lamp from the lean-to. "Better all get some sleep," he said.

Later, in the tiny lean-to, Hildy whispered to Ruby about Vernon's latest threat. Hildy finished by asking that tomorrow morning Ruby find some excuse to secure Hildy a minute alone with Ben.

Fearful of the danger posed by Vernon, Hildy softly prayed aloud, asking protection for all in the cabin. But the realization that she and all the others were in grave jeopardy kept her from sleeping even after Ruby dozed off. Hildy tried to reassure herself, because Ben had again tied the prisoner hand and foot to the stove.

Still, Hildy had no peace, so she again silently sent up petitions: *Lord, I had thought that moving to Flatsville was the worst thing that could happen. I couldn't stand the thought of leaving Ruby, Spud, Brother Ben, and all the others I love. But I was wrong. Being alive is what's important, and being with my family. They'll be frantic now because they don't know what's happened to us. The deputies Mrs. Armstrong was going to send apparently aren't coming. So please keep Vernon from carrying out his threat. Bring us all safely back to our families. Being together is far more important than where we live. We all want to be with our families at Christmas, wherever they are.*

A sense of peace finally came to her, and she slept.

She awakened to the sound of the recluse shaking down the stove grate prior to building up the fire. She sat up, the heavy homemade quilts falling from her shoulders.

*Tonight's Christmas Eve. Tomorrow's Christmas! I wonder if we can get home by tonight? But that depends on the weather, Buster, and Vernon.*

A strong glow filling the room drew Hildy's attention to the window. For a moment, she thought the brightness was the usual reflection off the snow. Then the realization hit her. *It's clearing! The storm's over!*

She hurriedly awakened her cousin and told her the news. "Get up!" Hildy urged excitedly. "Maybe we can save Buster and start back to the Armstrongs' today! If the roads are cleared, maybe we can get all the way to Lone River by tonight and have Christmas at home."

*Home!* Her hopes soared at the thought, then they plunged as she remembered. *My family has moved, so I don't even know what my home is like.* Then Hildy brightened, thinking, *But it doesn't matter where we live, just so we're together.*

The cousins entered the main cabin to join the others. Ruby asked Ben, "Do ye reckon we kin git home b'fore Christmas?"

He nodded. "I hope so."

"What about Buster?" Hildy asked.

Vernon snapped, "He's frozen solid by now."

The hermit rankled, saying sharply, "That shows how little you know about these mountains. It's a strange thing, but it has to warm up to snow. Oh, sure, sometimes we have blizzards with terrible winds and awful cold. But with clearing today, it'll be a lot colder tonight than it has been. I say we check on that horse and then send all of you home for Christmas."

Vernon snorted in derision. "Even if that horse is alive and you save him, he's so weak and crippled it'll take forever to get him down to a vet. So if everyone's so all-fired anxious to get home for Christmas, then forget the horse, and let's get started down the mountain."

Hildy felt her hopes sag, because she knew Vernon was right. She instantly felt a terrible mental tug between wanting Buster to be alive so he could be rescued, and knowing that if he were, Christmas would be spent in this desolate area with a murderer in their midst.

The hermit said calmly, "Ben and I have already worked that out. If Buster's alive—"

"Excuse me, Salty," the old ranger cut in, "but I think we'd better get a move on."

Hildy saw a flash of anger in the recluse's eyes, then it passed. "Time for talking later," he agreed.

While a hurried breakfast was prepared, Ruby managed to get Salter and Vernon away from Hildy so she could tell Spud and Ben about Vernon's latest threat.

When she had finished her hurried report, the old ranger observed, "I'm not surprised. My guess is that he'll wait until we've left Mr. Salter behind. I'm sure sorry you, Ruby, and Spud have to be involved, but I'll do all I can to keep the risks down."

Impulsively, Hildy suggested, "Why don't we ask Mr. Salter to come with us? He could spend Christmas at our house—" She stopped, remembering.

Spud said quickly, "I could invite him to go home with me. I'm sure Uncle Matt and Aunt Beryl would be glad to have him— well, if he took a bath first."

"He'd also be welcome at my place," Ben added. "So we'll ask him. But whether he comes with us or not, we must all keep a sharp eye on Vernon. He's certain to try escaping before we get to Quint's, where he'll be turned over to the authorities."

Hildy's stomach twisted with that scary knowledge. *Vernon has to try escaping today. If he does, then he'll carry out his threat, and none of us will ever see our families again.*

As Hildy started to turn away, the old ranger stopped her. "I just had an idea of how to deal with Vernon's threat."

"What's that?"

"It might not work if you knew," he said with a faint smile.

Ben and Hildy joined the recluse where he was slicing bacon from the rind. "Salty," the old ranger began, "we talked it over, and we want to invite you to come home with us for the holidays."

Hildy saw a sudden moist brightness in the hermit's eyes. He lowered them, saying only, "I'll think on it."

After breakfast, the party hurried across firm snow to the ridge above Buster's place of entrapment. By then, Hildy, walking with Ruby a few steps behind the three men and Spud, was alarmed at the sound of Ben's breathing. She started forward to check on him, when Vernon stopped.

"Bear tracks," he announced.

The others quickly gathered around. The recluse commented, "Must be a big old boar, judging from the size of those prints." He shaded his eyes with a hand against the sun's glare. "I told you those old boys sometimes come out of hibernation on warm days and just sort of wander about, like this one's doing."

"If he could smell us," Ben said thoughtfully, "he'd probably run away. But the wind's blowing the wrong way, from him to us, so unless he hears us, he may not know we're here."

The hermit scanned the countryside, adding, "Let's make some noise so we won't bump into him. I've stumbled across a couple of these old males in past winters, and they were mighty mean-tempered."

Hildy gripped Ruby's hand for comfort as everyone moved forward, tense and alert, talking loudly while following the bear's tracks, which showed he had stopped to turn over some large rocks. Farther on, a downed log showed long gashes where the bear had looked for grubs.

Hildy searched ahead, following the tracks, which had lost their meandering ways. "Look there," she said. "He's followed a straight line."

"Probably smelled something," Salter guessed. "He's going right for it."

"Horseflesh," Vernon said bluntly. "He got a whiff of your dead horse, Ben. Right now, he's probably—"

"Enough!" Ben said sharply. "Vernon, you drop back so Salty can keep an eye on you. You kids stay off to one side. I'll go take a look."

The rifle bolt clicked as the old ranger worked a cartridge into the firing chamber. But his breathing was so raspy that Hildy spoke up.

"Please, Brother Ben! You rest. I'll look."

"Thanks, but it'd be too dangerous."

"I'll go," Salter volunteered. "Only I'll trade this shotgun for your rifle."

As the men exchanged weapons, Hildy said, "Mr. Salter, I'd like to go with you."

He hesitated, then nodded. "Stay behind me."

Ruby and Spud also wanted to go, but the recluse shook his head. "One kid's enough. Come on, Hildy."

The bear tracks led straight up to the top of the ridge. There Hildy and the recluse stopped and craned their necks to see down the talus. In one quick glance, Hildy saw that Buster still stood, trapped exactly as she'd last seen him, except there were bear footprints behind him in the snow.

Hildy whispered, "He's not moving. But where's the bear?"

The hermit pointed. "After he wandered back and forth behind Buster, the bear went up that hill just this side of where the cliff starts. See where his tracks enter that manzanita? He's probably long gone."

Hildy nodded. "I'm glad he didn't try to hurt Buster." She turned to look again at the horse. He hadn't moved. She asked softly, "Is he . . . dead?"

" 'Fraid so."

A wave of sadness swept over Hildy. "Poor Buster!" I'm so sorry. Brother Ben'll be heartbroken."

"Can't blame him." Salter sighed. "Well, I hate to be the bearer of bad news, but let's go tell him."

As he turned around, Hildy sucked in her breath sharply. "Wait! I thought I saw Buster move."

"It's just your imagination."

Impulsively, Hildy announced, "I'm going down to make sure."

"Suit yourself. I'll wait here."

Hildy didn't dare allow her hopes to rise much, yet she found herself hoping as she neared Buster.

Suddenly, she heard something in the manzanita to her right. She stopped on the narrow trail just inches from the canyon's edge. Her heart jumped wildly while her eyes probed the dense underbrush.

With an angry roar, a huge black bear exploded from the brush and charged straight down hill toward Hildy!

# CHAPTER
## TWENTY-ONE

—

# DESPERATE MOMENTS

Hildy's scream seared her throat as the bear rushed toward her. She whirled around with a terrified sob to run up the treacherous talus trail. She heard the terrible clicking of his teeth mixed with short, puffing sounds. She recalled reading or hearing that a bear could outrun a horse for a short distance.

In terror, she realized, *Tomorrow's Christmas, but I'll not be here to—*

The thought was broken when her feet slipped on the snow and she fell hard. It happened so fast that she only partially thrust her mittened hands out to break her fall. At the same time, her feet shot out from under her. She slid backward toward the cliff's edge.

She frantically clawed at the snowy trail in a vain effort to stop herself, but it was too late. She felt her feet pass the canyon's rim. In that instant, her fingers grasped a white fir sapling growing there. She jerked to a head-snapping halt and clung there, legs dangling on nothing above the yawning chasm. Her upper body sprawled on the narrow trail. Her eyes widened in terror upon seeing the raging bear almost upon her.

She heard a sudden crash like thunder, and realized the hermit had fired the rifle.

The bear stopped inches from Hildy's head. She gazed fearfully at him. He rose on his hind feet to stare up the trail toward the crest. Hildy's eyes shifted to the ridge where the hermit knelt in the snow. Hildy heard the rattle of the bolt above Salter's muttered exclamations. The fired cartridge flipped out of the gun in a short arc. The bolt slid home on the second shell. The recluse threw the weapon to his shoulder and fired again.

The bear dropped to all fours and spun away from the helpless girl. With amazing speed, he raced up the hill by the cliff and plunged out of sight into the manzanita.

Salter called, "Hang on, Hildy! I'm coming!" He rushed recklessly toward her.

Hildy held on grimly as the hermit dropped the rifle, grabbed her wrists with both his hands and jerked hard. She sprawled safely on the snowy ledge as Ruby, Spud, Ben, and Vernon rushed toward her.

"You okay?" the recluse asked breathlessly.

She nodded, unable to speak. She glanced to where the bear had disappeared, then turned and looked with a shudder into the canyon where she had nearly fallen.

*Thanks, Lord! Maybe I'll be home for Christmas, after all—*

Her silent prayer broke off at the sight of Vernon. She had the feeling she could read his thoughts. *You escaped this time, but it's not over for you, or them.*

"Sorry to let that old bear get so close to you, Hildy," Salter apologized. "Unfamiliar gun, you know."

"I'm glad you didn't kill him."

"Didn't plan to do that," Salter explained. "A bear normally would run at the sight or scent of humans. But I guess that old boy thought you were threatening his food supply."

"Thanks," Hildy said, impulsively reaching up and giving her rescuer a quick kiss on his wild whiskers.

He squirmed in embarrassment, but Hildy quickly drew attention away from his discomfort by turning to speak to Ruby,

Spud, and Ben. She purposely avoided Vernon's menacing eyes.

When the others had finished exclaiming over the close call, Hildy told them why she'd gone down to check the horse. "I thought I'd seen him move, but must have been mistaken." She paused and laid her hand on the old ranger's. "I'm sorry." The words seemed so inadequate, so empty, though she meant it sincerely.

"Me too," the old ranger said quietly. "Buster deserved better than this after all he's been—"

He broke off so suddenly Hildy thought he was short of breath. "What's the matter?" she asked anxiously.

"He's alive!" Ben cried.

"Can't be," Vernon scoffed. "There's no way."

"Shh!" Hildy said with a severe frown. She turned toward the horse again and saw his head slowly rise. He whinnied softly to his master. "He is alive!" Hildy shouted joyfully.

"So what?" Vernon asked with a sneer. "It's too late to save him. I told you before: Even if you got him out of there, how far do you think he'd get on those hooves? And he's so weak he can't stand. Shoot him!"

"Shut up!" the recluse shouted, making his way down toward the horse. "I'll take a closer look, Ben."

Everyone was silent while the hermit made his inspection and came back. "He's in worse shape than before, but if we could get him up to my place, I could take care of him until a vet can be brought in."

Spud said, "If you do that, you won't be able to spend Christmas with us."

"I appreciate the invitation," the hermit answered, "but I've had about enough of being with people—even nice ones like all of you. I'd like my peace and quiet again. The horse'll keep me company if I need any."

Ben said, "I know we all want to get home tonight because it's Christmas Eve—"

Hildy broke in, "Of course we do! But what kind of memories would we have of this Christmas if we left Buster alone to die?"

Spud said, "Everything's in place: the pulley, the ropes, the collar. We'd only have to reposition the pry bar."

Ben's face puckered as though he were holding back tears. "Do you all agree?" Everyone nodded eagerly, except Vernon. "Then let's take our positions."

Hildy had mixed feelings of relief and concern as she picked up Buster's lead rope. She saw Ben carefully set the borrowed rifle against the cliff by the saddle and bridle. Hildy's gaze shifted to Vernon, whose gaze narrowed as he eyed the weapon.

But Hildy was reassured when Salter leaned his shotgun against the lodgepole pine where the pulley was attached. Ben could easily reach it before Vernon could get to the rifle. Satisfied, Hildy turned her attention to the final rescue attempt.

As before, Hildy's lead rope kept Buster's head up and facing the cliff. The rope collar ran from the horse's neck back to the white fir where Ben and Ruby waited. Spud, Salter, and Vernon had their backs about a foot from the canyon's edge. The prisoner's hands and feet had been untied so he could help with the pry bar.

Hildy nervously licked her lips, remembering how the pry bar had slipped before, throwing Spud, Ben, and Vernon off balance. Hildy shuddered, vividly seeing again how they had teetered on the edge of the canyon.

Ben called from the white fir, "Call it, Salty."

The old hermit waved acknowledgement and leaned his weight onto the pry bar. "Everyone ready?" When everyone answered affirmatively, Salter called out, "On three!"

Hildy's mittened fingers more firmly gripped Buster's lead rope as she said a quick, silent prayer.

" . . . Three!" the recluse cried. "Now!"

Hildy found herself straining inside, willing her weight to the men and boy as they threw their combined force on the pry bar.

For a long moment, nothing seemed to happen. Then Hildy let out a wild yell. "It's working!"

From the white fir, Ruby shouted gleefully, "It shore is! He's a-liftin' straight up!"

"Help me pull on this rope!" Ben said crisply. "If we don't take up the slack fast, he'll sink back again."

Hildy saw Ruby obey quickly—the doubled rope slid through the pulley until it stopped.

Ruby exclaimed, "We only gained about an inch!"

"But it's an inch we didn't have before!" Hildy shouted, feeling a rush of excitement. She raised her voice. "Mr. Salter! It's working! Buster's raised up a little, and the pulley kept him from sliding back."

"Then let's keep it going!" the hermit answered.

The process went on, slowly, tediously, while the sun climbed higher and the snow melted on the already slippery ledge. The horse was too weak to struggle or make a sound as the pry bar inched him up.

After a while, as Hildy watched the incredibly slow rescue, her mind became crowded with concern: *What if Buster falls over the cliff when he's tipped over? What if— Stop it!* she scolded herself. *Think about something else. Think about going on down the mountain this afternoon. Think about Christmas with the family, even if they've moved from Lone River.*

Salter's voice broke into her reverie. "He's up at about a forty-five degree angle, Ben. I know he's a dead weight on that pulley, but if it'll hold, one more good pry on this timber should do it."

Hildy's attention snapped back to Buster. His forequarters rose above the rocks that held him. His front legs dangled. He seemed to sag backward on his hind legs.

Ben called, "Hildy, you don't need to hold that lead rope anymore. We could use your help on this pulley so we can ease him over backward as gently as possible. Salty, you three had better reposition your bar so you're lifting up under the horse now, instead of prying down."

As Hildy scrambled to help, she heard Vernon's angry voice. "That means we'll have to stand right on the edge of the boulder! One slip, and we'll all end up at the bottom of that canyon like we almost did before!"

"There's no choice," the recluse replied evenly.

"I won't do it!" Vernon yelled.

"Then you're going into the canyon!" Salter shouted, grabbing Vernon by both arms.

"Okay! Okay!" Vernon cried. "I'll do it!"

Hildy sighed with relief, then smiled when the hermit winked and grinned at her, Ruby, and the old ranger. *Mr. Salter was bluffing!* Hildy decided.

When the pole was repositioned, Spud, Salter, and Vernon stood on the boulder and bent over the pry bar.

The hermit said, "I think one more time'll do it. Everybody ready?"

Hildy gave her full attention to the dramatic scene below. She strained with Spud, the hermit, and Vernon as they gave a mighty push down on the pry bar.

"He's going over!" Hildy shouted as the rope slackened in her hands. "He's starting to fall backward! O Lord, don't let him roll over the edge!"

For an instant, Buster seemed to sag toward the canyon, then he landed heavily on his hindquarters in the narrow trail, closer to the cliff than the canyon rim.

A mighty chorus of joyous yells echoed through the mountains as everyone rushed down to gather around the stunned horse. With an effort, he rolled onto his side, holding his head up but making no sound.

Hildy's eyes filled with tears. Everyone was safe, including Buster. The gallant old buckskin that had saved Ben's life years ago had now survived dangers from a mountain lion and bear, plus a snowstorm, cold, pain, hunger and thirst while held in a rock vice just inches from a sheer precipice. Now he was free!

Ben breathed hard but said between breaths, "The worst part's over. Now let's help him to his feet and get him back to your place, Salty."

"Nobody move!"

Vernon's harsh voice from behind made Hildy and the others spin around.

In the confusion, he had slipped away and picked up the rifle. "All of you—get over by the edge of the cliff! Now, move!"

# CHAPTER
## TWENTY-TWO

---

# THE UNFORGETTABLE GIFT

Hildy stared in sudden terror as Vernon repeated his command. "All of you get over there by the cliff!"

Nobody moved. Like Hildy, they seemed frozen in shock.

Hildy thought, *A moment ago we saved Buster's life, but now we're all going to lose ours. None of us will get home for Christmas!*

"Better do as he says." The hermit's voice reached through Hildy's spinning thoughts. Salter took a slow step away from the horse toward the cliff's edge.

"Do it fast!" Vernon thundered. "Move! Move!"

Silently, Hildy joined the others in stepping toward the yawning abyss at the edge of the trail.

She was tormented by the terrible realization of what was happening. *There must be some way to—*

Her desperate thoughts were interrupted by Vernon's words. "That's better. Now, old man, we have a debt to settle."

Hildy was surprised at how calm Ben seemed. "That's between you and me, Vernon. The others have nothing to do with it, so let them go."

"You know I can't do that."

The hermit shouted, "What kind of a man are you, Vernon? You can't hurt these kids! Their whole lives are ahead of them. Let them go!"

Vernon shook his head. "They're old enough to be witnesses. Now, Ben, since you started all this, I'm going to let you see it through to the end. You'll be the last. So, do you care where I start?"

Ben's soft drawl seemed unruffled. "I'm glad that Salty asked what kind of a man you are, because I've wondered all these years. I hoped you'd changed, but you haven't."

"That's enough!" Vernon's lips curled in a sneer. "Now, let's get this over with."

Ruby moaned, "Oh, I can't believe this is happenin'!"

Hildy reached out and pulled her cousin close, but said nothing. *What can I say?* Hildy asked herself in silent anguish. *All that I thought was important a couple of days ago isn't important at all. Not whether my family moved away from Lone River, not even the fact that I have no gift to put in the red box for Molly. Not even having a "forever" home. Just living is all that matters now.*

Spud touched Hildy's hand, then gave it a squeeze. The small, brief gesture touched Hildy so much that she suddenly felt like crying. *Oh, Spud! You'll never know how important you are to me!* she thought.

Standing on the canyon rim with five others on a beautiful day was a time for living and happiness, not tragedy.

Hildy's lips moved. *Lord, I've wanted my own way. I didn't want to move away. But I was wrong. Not my will, but Thine—*

Her prayer was left unfinished as a verse she'd learned in Sunday school came to mind. *Be careful for nothing; but in everything by prayer and supplication, with thanksgiving, let your requests be made known to God. . . .*

*To live!* she thought. *It doesn't matter where!* She opened her eyes as Vernon worked the rifle bolt.

The old ranger cleared his throat. "Uh, Vernon, you may want these."

Hildy blinked as Ben extended his closed right hand, then slowly turned it over and opened his fingers. Three brass rifle cartridges reflected in the morning sun.

Hildy gasped as she realized what that meant.

"Salty," Ben said in his slow, easy drawl, "I'd be obliged if you picked up your shotgun real fast. Vernon, I'll take that rifle back, because it's empty and therefore useless."

Vernon pulled the trigger, but there was only a metallic click.

The recluse let out a howl of laughter and retrieved his shotgun. "Vernon, you were a toothless tiger, only you didn't know it!"

The old ranger walked over and removed the rifle from the stunned man.

Ben explained, "Back at the cabin, Hildy warned me that Vernon had threatened to harm us. So after Salty scared off the bear and we traded guns again, I turned my back so nobody could see me unload the rifle. I set it where it'd be easy for Vernon to grab. I'm sorry to scare all of you, but I don't think Vernon will give us any more trouble."

The hermit said cheerfully, "Well, let's get Buster on his feet and on to my place. Then the rest of you had better hustle if you want to be home for Christmas."

With some difficulty, the gelding was helped to stand. Then, held up by his head, sides, and tail, Buster was aided on his slow, painful way to water, food, and attention to his wounds at the hermit's cabin.

When Buster was cared for in one of Salter's empty barns, Hildy solemnly looked into the recluse's eyes. "Mr. Salter, I hope you will visit us sometime."

He smiled through his wild crop of whiskers. "Maybe I'll do that when Buster gets well and Ben comes to take him to his friend's place."

"You think Buster will get well?"

"I'm sure of it." The recluse took one of Hildy's braids and gently tugged on it. "You ever going to cut these off?"

"Yes. When I get home, wherever that is, I'm going to do that."

"Good! The minute I laid eyes on you, I thought you were too old for braids. They're for little girls, and you're growing up."

"You think so?"

"I'm mighty sure of it."

"Thanks. Maybe that's why all that's happened in the last few days has made me realize some things that I didn't before. Life really means change. People and animals die. Fathers change jobs and kids change schools. People—like my family—move away from those they love."

"You'll make new friends," the hermit assured her.

Hildy smiled at him. "Yes, like you!"

He smiled back. "Thanks. You have to have a right attitude about change, Hildy. A person can make mistakes on how they react to change. I did that a long time ago, and ended up like this."

He paused, then added with a grin, "Oh, about the rat: I was just spoofing you. Adelle moved out a long time ago, but I never removed her nest. I'm sorry if I scared you girls with my made-up story."

Hildy smiled and said goodbye, then everyone started down the mountain.

They made good time for about half an hour before Hildy noticed the old ranger was having trouble breathing. She said she needed a rest, so everyone stopped.

Ruby, sitting on a fallen log, said, "Ben, ye never told us how Buster saved your life."

Hildy shot her cousin a warning look that the subject was a sensitive one, but the old ranger didn't seem to mind.

He said thoughtfully, "Well, I feel good about knowing Buster's going to live, and we'll soon turn Vernon over to the authorities. That'll remove the blot on my law-enforcement record.

Now I feel more comfortable talking about what happened way back then."

Vernon lifted his bound wrists and growled, "You better tell it right."

"You can correct me if I'm wrong, Vernon," Ben replied. He turned to look at Hildy, Ruby, and Spud. "Well, as I told you three earlier, I'd taken Vernon prisoner deep in the Texas brush country.

"We started back to ranger headquarters. I was riding Buster. Vernon, you were mounted on the horse stolen from my father. Then I made a mistake."

Vernon laughed nastily. "You sure did! You freed my hands after I told you I couldn't stay on that horse with my hands tied behind my back, not while we went through rattlesnake country. If one spooked my horse, I'd get bucked off and likely get bit myself. So you took off the handcuffs, and that's when I made my move.

"As you stepped back with the cuffs, I drove my spurs into the horse and yelled like an Apache. You tried to jump out of the way, but my horse's chest smashed into you, and you went down hard."

"Stunned me," Ben admitted ruefully.

"Sure did," the prisoner agreed. "While you were lying there, I grabbed your rifle and pistol and rode off. I didn't figure you'd be fool enough to try following me without a weapon."

"You didn't know us rangers," Ben replied in his slow, soft drawl.

Hildy prompted, "Then what happened?"

"When I came to my senses," Ben explained, "I dug out a hide-out revolver that I kept in my bedroll. Then I jumped on Buster and trailed Vernon by the prints the horse had left."

Vernon snorted. "I guess you thought I'd keep running hard, and ordinarily, that's what I would have done. But I got to worrying about leaving you alive. So I turned back, heard you coming, and just waited."

"Ambushed me while I had my eyes on the tracks," Ben acknowledged sadly.

"I thought I'd dropped you for good, using your own rifle," Vernon said bitterly. "It knocked you out of that saddle like you'd been pole-axed. When you didn't move, I rode on, figuring you were done for. That was my mistake, or you'd not have caught up with me all these years later."

"We rangers cast a long shadow," Ben answered.

Ruby asked, "But how did Buster save your life, Ben?"

He took a long, shuddering breath before answering. "The bullet broke my collarbone. I knew I'd die if I didn't get help, but there wasn't a house within a hundred miles that I knew about.

"Fortunately, Buster was always good about being ground-hitched, so he hadn't run off after I was shot out of the saddle. Somehow, with only one hand, and my shoulder hurting like crazy, I pulled myself up by the stirrups and finally managed to crawl onto Buster's back.

"But I was so weak that I couldn't sit up. So I loosened the reins, gave Buster his head, gripped the saddle horn with my good hand and lay along his neck. I kept passing out as he walked, but I was so mad at what Vernon had done to my father, and what I'd let happen to me, that I somehow managed to hang on.

"Finally, I heard voices and felt hands helping me out of the saddle. I opened my eyes and saw we were in a clearing with a small cabin by a little creek. Buster was drinking out of it when the young man and his wife who lived there helped me to the ground. They took me inside, cared for me as best they could, then stretched me out in a wagon and took me to the nearest doctor."

Ben paused, then added, "I never did figure out how Buster found the only other humans within miles of the ambush."

Vernon exclaimed, "That's easy! The horse must've smelled the water in that creek, and he was so thirsty he headed straight for it. You're just lucky those people lived there."

The old ranger nodded and stood up. "I guess that's possible, but I also figure the good Lord was looking out for me. Anyway, no matter how it happened, I'd have been dead if it hadn't been for Buster."

"Now," Hildy said softly, "he's alive because of you."

Everyone fell silent as they continued down the mountain toward the Armstrongs' place.

It was late afternoon on Christmas Eve when Hildy, Ruby, Spud, and Ben arrived with the Armstrongs' with Vernon in tow. They were welcomed by Quint and Martha with open arms. Deputies were called and they came at once to take Vernon into custody.

Spud phoned his "Uncle" Matt in Lone River to report what had happened. After he hung up, Spud turned to Hildy with a happy grin. "Fantastic news! Uncle Matt says your parents were so distraught about your being missing that they didn't move to Flatsville. They said they couldn't do that until they knew you were all right. So Uncle Matt said he'll make arrangements to have your family at Ben's when we arrive. Ruby's father will be there too."

After hot drinks and warm cookies, they all said their good-byes and season's wishes to the Armstrongs. Hildy was so cheered by the prospect of seeing her family and spending Christmas at home that she led the others in singing joyous Christmas carols on the drive back to the valley.

It was nearing midnight when Ben stopped the Packard at his ranch. Hildy's family, her uncle, and the banker's family, followed by Mischief, Hildy's raccoon, rushed forward to greet the late arrivals. Ruby's face lit up as Glenn Masters got out of the Farnham's car and smiled shyly at her.

Later, when Ben's house was filled with laughter and song, Ruby freed herself from her father's arms. She motioned for Hildy to come aside. Ruby looked across the room with shining eyes to where Glenn was talking to Spud.

Ruby whispered, "It's worth l'arnin'—learning—how to speak proper English. Isn't Glenn the cat's meow?"

Hildy laughed and hugged her cousin. "If you say so, but personally, I think Spud is."

Elizabeth approached the cousins. "There's a Christmas tree at home, all decorated with strings of popcorn, cranberries, and colored paper loops. And there's a basket of groceries. The church delivered them this morning. At first, Daddy's pride was hurt that he couldn't take care of us the way he wanted. But Molly whispered something to him, so he said thanks, nice and polite."

The mention of gifts made Hildy remember the one she had not been able to buy for Molly. Hildy couldn't tell anyone that she'd planned to buy something with the dollar her father had borrowed and been unable to repay.

It was the wee hours of the morning when the sleepy family came home from Ben's. Hildy slipped out to the barn and retrieved the red box she'd hidden there. Because there was no pretty ribbon around, Hildy tied the lid on with a piece of butcher's string.

She lay awake for a while, desperately trying to think of something, anything, she could put in the box. But nothing came to mind.

Around the small Christmas tree, in the morning, the five younger Corrigan children each received an orange, a few pieces of hard candy, and a small, inexpensive toy that Molly had hidden away months before. Hildy's gift was a plain white handkerchief. Yet it was the only Christmas gift Hildy would always remember.

When all the presents were unwrapped, Hildy reached for the empty red box. "Here," she said, embarrassed, handing it to her stepmother. "This is for you."

Hildy's four younger sisters crowded close as Molly carefully removed the lid. Hildy started to say, "I'll give you something later—" but Iola peered inside the box and cried, "It's empty!"

Molly reached out and hugged the five-year-old. "Oh, no, it isn't, Iola. I can see something in here."

Iola, Sarah, Martha, and even Elizabeth bent quickly to see what they had missed.

"Yes," Molly explained, her eyes shining as she turned to Hildy. "It's filled with love."

Molly and her stepdaughters were starting Christmas dinner when Brother Ben drove up in his big Packard. Hildy raced outside to talk to him alone for a moment.

"Brother Ben," she began breathlessly, "I've found the peace of God the pastor mentioned. I can move to Flatsville or wherever, knowing that it's not where I am now that's important, but where I'm going."

"I'm glad, Hildy," he replied.

Hildy rushed on, "I'll always have great memories of friends and the happy times we've had together. And I certainly hope we'll meet again. Eventually, with God's help, I'll become a teacher, and have the 'forever' home I want for my family and myself."

The old ranger nodded. "Through faith in God, it is possible to face whatever changes life sends along. Remember that."

Hildy wanted to say more, but the rest of her family came streaming out, inviting their guest inside.

"Much obliged, but I can't stay," he said. "However, I will step inside out of the cold for a minute."

When Ben was seated in the living room, he explained, "I want to tell all of you about some phone conversations I've had today. The first was with a rancher who lives near me. He called to say one of his riders had unexpectedly quit, and did I know where another rider could be found on short notice? Joe, I told him I'd have you look him up first thing tomorrow."

Hildy shouted with joy, but the old ranger held up his hand. "Wait. I haven't told you about the other phone calls. When my son and daughter called long distance to wish me a joyous Christmas, I told them everything that's been going on lately. I hadn't planned to tell them about my health until later, because I didn't want to spoil their holiday. But I changed my mind after what's happened in the last few days.

"I told my kids that I was so touched by the example of my horse that wouldn't die that I've decided to fight this cancer and stick around as long as I can. That way I'll be able to enjoy family and friends, and sometime visit Quint and Martha again, and Buster and Salty. Now, my kids are coming to see me as soon as they can, and they're bringing all my grandchildren!"

"Oh, Brother Ben!" Hildy said with a break in her voice. "I'm so glad for you!"

"There's more," he said in his easy drawl. "My children said they're happy where they live now, and they're fairly comfortable financially. So even though I've decided to take a smaller place in town, they said I could do whatever I wanted with my ranch. I want to offer it to you folks to live there, rent free, until all six of you kids are out of high school." He looked at Hildy. "You can keep your raccoon, plant a garden, have a dairy cow—"

Hildy's gasp and Molly's stifled sob briefly interrupted the old ranger, then he continued, "It's not a 'forever' home, but it's at least a place to let down roots. What do all of you say to that?"

Hildy shouted, and rushed to join the others in hugging the old ranger, while familiar words leaped to her mind: *"Be careful for nothing, but in everything by prayer . . . and the peace of God, which passeth all understanding. . . ."*

Aloud, Hildy whispered, "It's not only going to be a very good Christmas and bright new year; it's going to be a wonderful life!"

And it was—for Hildy, her family, Ruby, Spud, and all her other friends.